THE
DATING
GAME

a novel by Natalie Standiford

LITTLE, BROWN AND COMPANY

New York ✦ Boston

Little, Brown and Company
Time Warner Book Group
1271 Avenue of the Americas, New York, NY 10020
Visit our Web site at www.lb-teens.com

Interior created and produced by Parachute Publishing, L.L.C.
156 Fifth Avenue
New York, NY 10010

ISBN: 0-316-11040-X

10 9 8 7 6 5 4 3 2 1

CWO

Printed in the United States of America

For René, Biz, Darcey, and Hawes

1 What Color Is Your Love Aura?

To:	mad4u
From:	Your daily horoscope

HERE IS TODAY'S HOROSCOPE: VIRGO: You will embark on a life-changing project today. Try not to screw it up.

I love Sean Benedetto.

I, Madison Markowitz, love Sean Benedetto.

Madison Emily Markowitz loves Sean [?] Benedetto.

(*What is Sean's middle name? Must find out in order to prepare wedding announcement.*)

Why do I love Sean Benedetto? Let me count the top five reasons:

1. *His hair rocks, especially the way it sticks up in the back.*

2. *The bump on his nose is sexy.*

3. *He's graceful but in a totally boyish way.*

4. *His voice . . . I can't describe it but if you poured honey on*

a hot sandy beach and then went surfing, that's sort of it.

5. He hardly ever looks at me but when he does his brown eyes look like chocolate puddles and I want to dip myself in them.

Madison's teacher, Dan Shulman, cleared his throat, and she thought she'd better throw some attention his way. "I hope everybody had a good holiday," Dan said. "You're all looking a little bleary this afternoon."

Fifth period Friday, the end of the first week after Christmas vacation. Who wouldn't look bleary? And Interpersonal Human Development, in spite of being a long, stupid name for sex ed, wasn't exactly a shot of espresso.

Pay attention, Mads! Or big bad Dan will yell at you!

Holly Anderson, one of Mads' two best friends, scrawled that in Mads' notebook and flashed her a wicked grin. Holly wasn't paying attention herself—she was secretly doing her Spanish homework. Lina Ozu, Mads' other best friend, reached over and scribbled, *He will not! Dan never yells.*

"Girls, are you with us?" Dan said.

Mads straightened up. She and Holly and Lina nodded. "Good."

Uh-oh—yelled at by Dan. (For him, that was yelling.) Mads stole a glance at Lina, whose face had gone code red. This must be killing her. She had a monster crush on Dan, almost as big as Mads' for Sean.

See, I told you you'd get in trouble, Holly scribbled. Mads batted her hand away.

"If you remember, this semester we're doing independent study projects," Dan said. "In this class we've focused mostly on the, uh, special relationship between a man and a woman, or a guy and a girl, or sometimes two guys or two girls . . . " Dan seemed to stumble over the many possible combinations, embarrassed, but he recovered. "Now you're going to discover how those human dynamics work in real life."

A "whoo" erupted in class, followed by nervous laughter. "I'm going to check out Rebecca's human dynamics," Karl Levine called out. Rebecca Hulse laughed along with everyone else. Nothing seemed to ruffle her.

To Mads, Rebecca was like a mosquito bite on the sole of her foot—irritating yet impossible to ignore. How could she exist in real life? She was smart and skinny and rich and golden-pretty and good at sports and people liked her. Rebecca seemed to belong to a secret race of supergirls. Mads couldn't figure out where they came from but she wanted to be one *so badly*.

"That's not what I mean," Dan said. "Social dynamics, for instance, are one aspect of being human. Can anyone think of a good example?"

Nobody moved.

"Remember, we talked about this before Christmas," Dan said. "Do men and women tend to behave differently in social situations? Such as . . . ?" His voice rose, inviting the class to respond. "Anyone?"

Ramona Fernandez raised her ring-covered, black-taloned hand. "On the road. You could analyze the driving records of men and women and see who gets more speeding tickets."

"Thank you, Ramona," Dan said. "That would be a good idea for a project. Another example might be lunchtime behavior. What food choices do guys and girls make? Where do they sit in the lunchroom? . . ."

Blah-blah, blah-blah, blah . . .

Mads wouldn't have thought a goth chick like Ramona, who dyed her hair black, painted her face ghost-white, and wore nothing but filmy Morticia Addams gowns, would go for being teacher's pet. Just goes to show. Ramona was almost as postal over Dan as Lina was.

There was something very Rosewood about a goth-rebel-teacher's pet. Rosewood School for Alternative Gifted Education, or RSAGE, was a magnet school for gifted students. Its approach to education was "experimental," which meant, as far as Mads could tell, lots of independent study and calling your teachers by their first names. You had to pass a test to get in, but in Carlton Bay, California, the test didn't weed out many kids. Carlton Bay was one of those towns where every kid's a genius—at least as far as their parents were concerned. And if you weren't born brilliant, you learned to fake it.

"You can work in teams or alone," Dan said. "I'll need to see a project proposal by next Friday and a progress report every week after that. After eight weeks you'll do a final paper describing the results of your research. That means your paper is due right before spring break. Got it?"

Mads nodded at Lina and Holly. It was understood they were a team. The question was, what would they do for their project?

We'll figure it out at my house tonight, Holly scribbled in the margin of Mads' notebook.

X-l-ent, Mads scribbled back. Friday night at Holly's. It was becoming a tradition. But only because none of them ever had anything better to do.

"Where are Curt and Jen tonight?" Mads asked Holly. "Dinner party?"

The three girls settled in front of the fire in Holly's great room, which was big yet cozy, like the lodge at an expensive ski resort. They were eating pizza and drinking a bottle of red wine Holly had swiped from her parents' cellar. Not that the Andersons cared. They believed that teenagers should be allowed to drink at home, in moderation, like Europeans. That's what Mads loved about the Andersons—they were so different from her own parents, who veered wildly from overprotective to overindulgent, depending on the child-rearing trend of the moment.

"Curt's out of town. Jen's at the opera," Holly said. "And Piper went to meet some college friends in the city. We've got the place to ourselves until at least one or two in the morning." Piper, Holly's older sister, was a freshman at Stanford and still home for winter break.

Mads had met Lina and Holly a year and a half earlier, as freshmen at RSAGE. Lina and Holly had been friends since first grade, but Mads went to a different elementary school. She was nervous about starting at RSAGE—her best friend from middle school went to a private school instead. She saw Holly and Lina together and had a feeling about them, kind of like love at first sight. She marched up to them—she wasn't shy—and said, "You two are missing something. What you need is a third wheel." They laughed, and that was that. Friends.

"*We* should be out," Mads complained. "I can't believe we've got nothing to do on a Friday night *again*. Why isn't anyone having a party?"

"Someone probably is," Lina said. "We just weren't invited." Lina's long black hair gleamed in the firelight. She was slender, medium-tall, Japanese-American, with a sweet oval face. At first Mads thought she seemed cool and reserved, but it wasn't long before she knew the real Lina—a smart girl struggling to keep her passions under control. Mads was emotional, too, but it never occurred to her to try to control it.

"Why wouldn't we be invited? That sucks." Mads took a sip of wine and her cheeks immediately flushed red. Wine did that to her, she was learning. Mads and Lina were both fifteen, but Mads looked younger, short and cute with fine black hair to her shoulders, a freckled snub of a nose, and small, sleepy blue eyes.

"We're supposed to be figuring out what to do for our IHD project, anyway," Holly said. She stoked the fire. She was good at practical stuff like that—building fires, cooking, giving sensible advice. She didn't *look* practical, with her long, wavy blond hair and curves like the hairpin turns on the Pacific Coast Highway. She was as busty as Mads was flat. Mads sometimes called her "the Boobmeister" just to tease her.

"How about interviewing our parents?" Lina suggested. "We could compare and contrast the way they dated with dating now."

"Believe me, you don't want to get my mom started on that," Mads said. "She gets all goopy and talks about Dad as if he were some kind of sex god. Which I'd rather not think about."

"You come up with something then, Mads."

Mads nibbled on a pizza crust. "I don't know, we could make an art project out of tampons or something."

"Gross," Lina said.

Mads drained her glass. "This wine is making me warm. But I like it." She waved her glass at Holly. "Dump a little more in here please, Boobmeister."

Holly poured more wine into each girl's glass. "Come on, you guys, think!"

Three minutes of silence followed. Mads strained her brain, trying to come up with a good idea.

"Anything?" she asked the others. They shook their heads.

"Maybe we're trying too hard," Mads said. "My mother always says, 'The truth appears when you stop searching for it,' or something like that." Mads knew she hadn't gotten it quite right. "Or maybe, 'When you stop looking for answers, the answers find you.'"

"Your mom's such a zen-head," Holly said. "Do you think an idea is just going to drop out of the sky?"

"That happens sometimes," Lina said.

"All right, we'll let the answer find us," Holly said. "But it better find us before next Friday. I'm going to check my e-mail."

Mads and Lina followed Holly to her room. Holly checked her e-mail—nothing but spam. She was about to log off when Mads said, "Let's check our horoscopes. They have good ones on girlworld."

All three girls subscribed to a web site called Your Daily Horoscope, which e-mailed them their personalized forecasts every day, but it didn't hurt to get a second opinion.

Holly found the girlworld Web site. Before she had a chance to click on "Horoscopes" a colorful pop-up caught Mads' eye.

New Quiz! What Color Is Your Love Aura?

"Let's take that quiz," Mads said. "I have no idea what color my love aura is."

"When are they going to stop making up new auras?" Holly said. "There's your love aura, your friendship aura, your shopping aura, your homework aura, your shoe aura . . ."

"Let's just take the quiz," Lina said. Holly clicked and up came the first question.

WHAT COLOR IS YOUR LOVE AURA?

1. **To you, a good kiss is:**

    A A peck on the cheek

   B Lip to lip with a tight pucker

   C Lip to lip with a little tongue play

   D Nice and wet with lots of tongue

"Pick 'd,'" Mads said.

"Ew," Holly said. "I hate super-wet kisses."

"You don't like them either, Mads," Lina said.

"I know," Mads said. "But what happens if you pick the grossest answers? What color is the love aura of someone who likes super-wet kisses? I have to know." The wine had made her a little tipsy, and this suddenly seemed like an important issue.

Holly clicked "d." "Okay," she said. "An experiment. What color is the grossest love aura?"

2.
Your idea of a hot date is:

A ▶ Dinner with your parents

B ▶ A stroll and a stop for a cup of coffee

C ▶ A movie with an easy-to-follow plot for plenty of makeout action

D ▶ Getting a motel room

"'D' again," Mads urged. "I see where this is going." She'd taken a few magazine quizzes in her time. "All the sexiest answers are going to be 'd.'"

"Your wish is my command." Holly clicked "d."

"Can we take this quiz again later and pick our real answers?" Lina asked.

"What would your real answer be?" Holly asked.

Lina reread the answers to number two. "Well, none of those is my idea of a hot date," she said. "I'd like to go out to dinner. Or maybe a *good* movie, not a bad one."

"Next question," Mads said.

3.

Your favorite pickup line is:

A   **What're you looking at?**

B   **Hi. What's your name?**

C   **You're cute. What are you doing for the rest of my life?**

D   **Shut up and kiss me.**

"See, I'd never say any of those lines to a boy," Mads said. "We might as well pick 'd' again for fun."

4.

You're eating with a guy and he spills ketchup on his shirt. You:

A   **Say nothing**

B   **Wipe it off with your napkin**

C   **Lick it off**

D   **Tell him his shirt has ketchup on it, then rip it off**

"That's just ridiculous," Holly said as she clicked on "d."

5.

You'll dump a guy if:

A   **He doesn't say "Please" and "Thank you"**

B   **He swears too much**

C   **He's got butt zits**

D   **He won't do "everything"**

"Guys get zits on their butts?" Mads asked. "And what do they mean, 'everything'?"

"You know what everything means, Mads," Holly said. "You just don't know you know it."

They finished the quiz, answering "d" on every question.

"Now we just fill in a screen name and submit to get our answers," Mads said, taking over for Holly at the keyboard. Under "name" she typed in "Boobmeister Holly" as a joke.

"Yuk yuk yuk." Holly did her sarcastic spaz laugh.

Mads pressed SUBMIT and they waited a few seconds for their quiz to be analyzed.

ANSWER KEY:

If you picked mostly A's, your sexual aura is WHITE. Face it, you're a prude. Join a convent now!

If you picked mostly B's, your aura is YELLOW. You're cautious, maybe too much so. Time to take a few chances.

If you picked mostly C's, your aura is BLUE. You're sensuous and sexy but don't carry it too far—most of the time. Be careful.

If you picked mostly D's, your aura is RED. You're a total slut! You might want to slow down a bit. But hey, maybe it works for you.

Boobmeister Holly: YOU PICKED ALL D'S. Your aura = red. Red = slut.

"Happy now, Mads?" Holly asked.

"Yes," Mads said. "Now I know that the grossest love aura is red and that we're all sluts."

"Speak for yourself!" Lina bonked her with a pillow.

Mads noticed an icon at the bottom of the quiz: E-MAIL THIS TO A FRIEND. "Let's send this to somebody," she said. She thought of Rebecca Hulse. Would she think this was funny? If she did, they could laugh about it together at school on Monday. Mads might get to know her a little better, and that would get her closer to finding out the secrets of the supergirls.

"Does Rebecca like quizzes?" she asked Lina. Of the three of them, Lina knew Rebecca best. They played field hockey together.

"Yeah, I guess so," Lina said.

"So let's send it to her," Mads said.

"Why?" Holly asked.

"For fun," Mads said. She forwarded the quiz, funny answers, "Boobmeister Holly" and all.

Lina glanced at the clock. "It's almost midnight already. Weren't we supposed to do some kind of homework-type thing tonight?"

"Our IHD project," Holly said. "Any ideas drop out of the sky yet?"

"No," Lina said.

"It might take a few days," Mads said.

"I'll keep an eye out for UFOs," Holly said.

But the answer, when it came, didn't drop out of the sky. It came from cyberspace, where anything could happen—and did.

2 Meet the Boobmeister

To:	hollygolitely
From:	Your daily horoscope

HERE IS TODAY'S HOROSCOPE: CAPRICORN: Don't bother getting up today. Really. I'm so totally serious.

H i, Holly," Keith Carter said as Holly headed for her locker first thing Monday morning. "I mean, Boo —"

"Shut up!" Derek Scotto elbowed Keith in the ribs, hard. They both cracked up.

Holly had a familiar sinking feeling. There was something sinister in the air. The school was buzzing with it— vicious gossip molecules infecting everyone who breathed them. She'd been there before, the butt of the jokes, the subject of whispers, the recipient of fake smiles. But why was it happening now? What were they saying this time? And what had set it off?

All right, calm down. Maybe she was overreacting. After all, Keith and Derek were idiots, and everyone knew it.

"Hey, Holly—my shirt has ketchup on it." A skinny kid about half Holly's height leered and flapped his tongue at her. His friends clustered around him, egging him on. "Want to rip it off?"

Okay, so she wasn't overreacting. *Stupid ninth-grader.* Holly didn't even know his name. But he knew hers. *Great.*

Holly stopped and loomed over the kid. "Sorry, I don't understand what you're talking about. I forgot my English-to-Dork dictionary."

"Ha ha, dork." The boy shrank away, his friends taunting him. That took care of that, for now.

It hadn't been this bad since eighth grade, when some boy wrote "I felt up Holly" on the bathroom wall. Another boy added, "Me, too. Holly has supertits." Before she knew it, everyone was not-so-secretly calling her "Jolly Holly Supertits" behind her back. It didn't stop until Kayla Ashton walked out of the girls' bathroom with the back of her skirt tucked into her thong. Thank god. Then everybody forgot about Jolly Holly and went after Kayla Asscrack.

Holly had developed before any other girl in her class. She finished fifth grade a flat-chested little girl, spent that summer growing out of all her clothes, and by the time sixth grade started she was busty as a Barbie doll. It was a shock for everybody, especially her. But that was five years ago, and she was used to her body now. What was taking everybody else so long?

She came upon a clump of girls, including Rebecca Hulse, who leaned against the wall, sharp knees and elbows jutting out like spikes. They were whispering and giggling. They stopped when Holly approached, but she caught the last little hiss.

"Did you read the answers she gave? Oh my god. She was rated a total slut!"

So that was it. The love-aura quiz. And Mads' stupid joke name, "Boobmeister Holly." Holly silently vowed never to pull an EWI—E-mailing While Intoxicated— again. And Mads was going to get it.

"Hey, Holly." Rebecca's lips cracked apart, showing her white teeth. Holly supposed it was meant to be a smile. She'd never had a problem with Rebecca before, though she wasn't as relaxed around her as Lina seemed to be. But now she felt wary.

"I was just telling everyone how that quiz you sent me was only a joke," Rebecca said. "Some people actually thought you meant it seriously! Can you believe that?"

Holly's brain tried sending relaxing signals to her face muscles, but her face muscles were not feeling cooperative.

"It was a goof," Holly explained. "Mads and Lina and

I got a little tipsy and we were just fooling around—"

"I knew it," Rebecca said too brightly. "That's what I keep telling everybody!"

"The weird thing is, how does everybody know about it?" Holly asked. "We only forwarded it to you, Rebecca, not the whole school."

"I know," Rebecca said. "But it was so funny I had to send it to Autumn. How did I know she was going to paste it onto her blog?"

Her blog! "Nuclear Autumn." The whole school read Autumn Nelson's blog. It was a neverending source of gossip, sniping, and drama-queen hysterics. How would Holly ever get out of this? Could she pay Kayla to parade around in her underwear again?

"I'm really sorry, Holly," Rebecca said. "I never meant for this to happen—I swear!"

"That's funny," Holly said. "I thought you had total control over your minions."

Rebecca's friends looked horrified, but Rebecca herself didn't break a sweat. "Come on, Holly, Autumn's my friend, but I can't control what she does."

Holly wasn't so sure. The whispering began again as she walked away. Rebecca was hard to read. Was she trying to embarrass Holly on purpose? Was she covering for Autumn or just being mean? Holly knew it didn't matter. These things took on a life of their own.

She found a note taped to her locker.

Dear Boobmeister, If Nick Henin can have you, why not me? I was in line ahead of him. Smooches, Bastiano

Holly grimaced. Bastiano, otherwise known as Sebastiano Altman-Peck, had the locker next to hers and liked to tease her.

She glanced at the note again. Nick Henin? What was that supposed to mean? Holly knew who he was—every girl did, he was that cute—but she'd never said a word to him. A great soccer player, he had famously quit the team sophomore year "out of boredom."

Holly crumpled up the note just as its author, Sebastiano, slinked toward her, and flicked open his locker.

Holly tossed the ball of paper in his face. "You're such a wit, Bastiano."

"I know. So just tell me. How did you do it?"

"Do what?"

"Bag Nick Henin. Don't play innocent with me, Anderson. It's all over school."

"What?" Holly tried to catch her breath. "What's all over school? I mean, besides that 'Boobmeister' crap."

"You and Nick. Nice touch, by the way. The nick-name, I mean. Classy with a capital K."

Holly squeezed her eyes shut. "That was Mads' idea. We were just kidding around. I never meant for the whole school to read it. And I never mentioned Nick. What are they saying?"

"I read on 'Nuclear Autumn' that you and Nick hooked up over Christmas break. Apparently he couldn't get enough of your smokin' bod, Boobmeister."

"Stop calling me that," Holly snapped. Her mind raced. What should she do? Nick was a catch—it was no shame to have dated him. In fact, it might be a good thing. Sort of a status symbol. Holly wasn't sure. But maybe it was best to keep her mouth shut until she sorted this thing out. Nobody would believe her if she denied it, anyway.

"Who started this?"

Sebastiano shrugged. "Anonymous posting. Who knows where these things come from? What's the matter? Isn't it true?"

Holly tried to cover her nausea with a mysterious half-smile. At least she hoped it looked mysterious. "What does Nick say?"

Sebastiano popped two pieces of gum into his mouth. "I'll ask him next chance I get. Nicky and I are like *that*." He wrapped one finger around another and held them up for her to see. Then he slammed his locker shut.

He slinked away, notebooks at his hip. Halfway down the hall he turned and called, "Later, Boobalicious."

Holly banged her forehead against the flimsy metal of her locker door—once, twice, three times. Weren't her classmates supposed to be too mature for this stuff, the name-calling, the ridiculous rumors? The answer: No.

"Holly, stop!" Mads called from down the hall. "You'll give yourself brain damage!" She and Lina raced to Holly's side.

"Are you okay?" Lina asked. "There's no need for headbanging. This will pass."

"I guess you heard the rumors," Holly said. "Mads, why did you have to send that stupid quiz to Rebecca?"

"I'm sorry!" Mads cried. "I didn't know she'd spread it all over the school. Has anyone said anything to you?"

"Oh, no," Holly snapped. "Every guy in school thinks I'm looser than my grandmother's neck—*before* the facelift."

"It's not really Mads' fault, Holly," Lina said. "Autumn's the one who posted the quiz on her blog."

"Holly, you were there. You thought it was funny, too." Mads said. Her eyes were damp. Holly wished she hadn't snapped at her. It was hard to stay mad at Mads. And anyway, she was right.

"It's okay, Mads," Holly said. "I still think it's funny. I just wish everyone else could be cooler about it."

"You know what you need?" Lina said. "A nice big cup of hot cocoa. Or maybe a latté. Let's go to Vineland this afternoon."

"Sounds good," Holly said. "Too bad I have to get through a whole day of school first."

• • •

"Maybe Nick made the anonymous posting himself," Madison said. She blew on her coffee and took a sip.

Holly, Lina, and Madison had snagged a prime window table at Vineland, a café in a tiny wooden cottage on Rutgers Street, overlooking the valley. Carlton Bay was a pretty town, bordered on the west by a small bay, with a marina and funky shops and seafood restaurants. From there the town spread across miles of woods dotted with houses to a lush green valley. The girls stared out the window but barely saw the landscape. Their minds were otherwise occupied.

"You know what I heard today?" Mads said. "I was late for gym and these two juniors were in the locker room. They were talking about some girl named Krista and how she went out with two boys who were friends."

"At the same time?" Lina asked.

"No. First she went out with one, and after they broke up she went out with his best friend. She said they both kissed exactly the same way, as if they learned it from the same person."

"Ew," Lina said. "That's weird."

"And then Jen and her friend were talking about how weird boys look when they're naked," Mads said. "All lumpy. I mean, how many naked boys have you seen? They made it sound like naked boys are selling candy door-to-door."

"It's just talk," Holly said. "Everybody acts as if they

know what they're talking about, but they really don't."

"It sure sounds like they know what they're talking about," Mads said. "I couldn't have made that stuff up."

"Did they know you were there?" Lina asked.

"Not at first," Mads said. "But then they heard me and stopped talking. And when they saw me they asked me where we found that love quiz, because they wanted to try it. I was surprised they knew who I was."

"Lots of people asked me about the quiz, too," Lina said. "I mean, when they weren't gossiping about—"

"Don't finish that sentence," Holly said. "I must have been called 'the Boobmeister' about a hundred times today."

Which sent a hundredth pang of guilt through Mads. "I'm so sorry about the whole Rebecca thing," she said.

They looked up to see Rebecca Hulse making her way toward them. Holly steeled herself for more fakey-fakey nice-nice.

"Here she comes," Mads whispered.

Rebecca flipped a long hank of blond hair over her shoulder and leaned her hands on their table. Her white shirt was unbuttoned just enough to show a peek of a pink lace bra underneath. Mads made a mental note to buy a button-down shirt and a pink lace bra as soon as possible.

"Holly, I hope you're okay," Rebecca said. "I'm really sorry. I wanted to say it again—I'm so sorry about this whole thing. I swear I never meant for that quiz to get around the way it did."

She glanced back meaningfully at Autumn, who sat near the fireplace facing the other way.

"It's no big deal, Rebecca," Holly said. "It's given me a chance to work on my snappy comebacks. I was getting rusty."

"Just as long as you don't hate me," Rebecca said.

"I don't hate you," Holly said. *I just don't like you that much,* she added to herself.

"Thank god," Rebecca said. "Because I really like you, all you guys, and I don't want anything to get in the way of us being friends." She started to walk away, but stopped to add, "By the way, nice work bagging Nick Henin. Okay, see you later."

They watched her walk away and sit down with Autumn. Mads tried to read the label on her jeans.

"Okay, Lina," Holly said. "You're Rebecca's teammate. You know her best. Sincere or insincere?"

Lina knew a side of Rebecca the other girls never saw. They were both good hockey players, and they worked well together on the field. Rebecca could be snotty, but that wasn't the way Lina knew her. "I think sincere," Lina said. "Why would she want to hurt you?"

Mads squinted at Rebecca and Autumn huddled across the room. Mads didn't necessarily *like* Rebecca. She envied her. "Hmmm, I vote insincere. You know what? I bet she's jealous! She's hot for Nick! That must be it."

"That doesn't make sense," Lina said. "That rumor didn't come out until after Autumn posted the quiz on her blog."

"Oh, right. Never mind." Mads paused, opened her mouth, shut it, opened it again, and shut it again.

"Mads, do you want to share?" Holly asked.

"When did you sleep with Nick Henin?" Mads asked. "And why didn't you tell us?"

"I didn't—" Holly began.

"It was at Ingrid's Christmas party, right?" Lina said. "You disappeared for almost an hour."

"Yeah," Mads said. "I always wondered what happened to you that night, and you never really explained it. But you must have been fooling around with Nick!"

Oh yes, Ingrid's Christmas party. Holly remembered it well. The thing is, she didn't recall Nick being there. And she hadn't realized she'd been gone for so long. All she was doing was sitting in Ingrid's mother's bathroom reading an article about Gwyneth Paltrow in *Vanity Fair*.

"I can't believe how cool you are," Mads said. "You fool around with a cute senior like Nick and don't even say anything?"

"No, see, the thing is—"

"Look at Rebecca and Autumn," Mads interrupted.

"See the way they're talking? It's driving them crazy!"

"Can I please finish a sentence? I didn't sleep with Nick Henin," Holly said.

"You didn't?" Mads was confused. How could so many rumors be wrong? "So you just made out a little?"

"I've hardly spoken to him," Holly said. "We didn't even kiss. Nothing. Nada. Zero. Zip."

"Huh." Mads still couldn't believe it. When it came to the truth, she generally preferred the most exciting version, and this wasn't it.

"Then why is everybody saying that you did?" Lina asked.

"God only knows," Holly said. "People like to make up stories about me for some reason."

"I think you should take it as a compliment," Lina said. "It's like a talent."

"I do," Holly said. "What choice do I have?" She was getting impatient. All this talk bothered her more than she wanted anyone to know. "Can we change the subject now? Did any fabulous IHD ideas dropped out of the sky and land in your breakfast cereal this morning?"

The table went silent. After a few minutes Mads began to think out loud. Sometimes this got her into trouble, but sometimes, she found, it was the only way to solve a problem.

"Let's say Nick started this rumor about you," she

said. "Why would he do it? Because boys are obsessed with sex! They can't help themselves. Sex talk burbles out of them against their will."

"It does?" Lina said.

"How else do you explain it?" Mads said. "They say so many stupid things that don't make sense. And girls are nice and calm and rational."

"Sure they are," Holly said. "What's your point?"

"Everybody knows boys are more into sex than girls," Mads said. "Our IHD project will prove it. We can set up our own blog, like Autumn's, just for this project. We'll take a poll of the students. We'll ask all kinds of questions, how experienced they are, what they like to do on dates, whatever we want to know. And we'll use that information to prove that boys have sex on the brain more than girls."

"We can make it like a quiz," Lina said. "Like that love aura quiz we filled out, only better."

"But what would the subject of the quiz be?" Holly asked.

"'Are You Obsessed with Sex?'" Mads said.

"And then what?" Holly said. "People will just answer Yes or No? That's not much of a project."

"We can expand it," Mads said. "Make it a matchmaking quiz. That way we'll get lots of responses, and they'll be more honest."

"But then everyone will expect us to match them up with people," Lina said.

"So we will!" Mads said. "It will be fun. And we can save the best boys for ourselves!"

"You're an evil genius, Mads," Holly said. "We'll analyze the quiz answers and prove our hypothesis. Then we can write it all up in fakey scientific language so Dan will think it's some kind of earth-shaking discovery."

"Maybe we *will* make a discovery," Lina said. "Maybe we'll really learn something about the kids we go to school with."

"Sure," Holly said. "And maybe 'Nuclear Autumn' will win the Nobel Prize for Literature."

But secretly, Holly hoped Lina was right. What was really going on in people's minds? The minute she hit puberty—and got the bod—everyone's attitude toward her changed. Why? Did they know something she didn't? Did the way her body looked really make her different from everybody else?

Holly was skeptical. But if this project could answer those questions, it really would be a gift from above.

3 Sex on the Brain

To:	linaonme
From:	Your daily horoscope

HERE IS TODAY'S HOROSCOPE: CANCER: Stop obsessing, Cancer! No, your head isn't shaped funny, your feet aren't gigantic, and your teeth are plenty white. Yes, something is wrong with you. But not that.

Class: Interpersonal Human Development
Teacher: Dan Shulman
Date: Friday, January 21
Proposal for "The Dating Game: Sexual Attitudes Among RSAGE Students in Carlton Bay, California"
by Holly Anderson, Madison Markowitz, and Lina Ozu
Sex on the brain: Who's more obsessed, boys or girls?

Our hypothesis: Boys think about sex more than girls. To

prove it, we will create a special Web log with restricted access—open only to RSAGE students—containing a questionnaire entitled "The Dating Game." Students will answer questions about their sexual attitudes and experiences. To encourage participation, we will set up the Web site as a matchmaking service and actually match people up with dates. We hope these dates will provide still more data to support our hypothesis.

After eight weeks we will analyze the data and draw conclusions. Are boys more sex-crazed than girls? Our final paper will answer this question and silence the debate once and for all.

p.s. Oh, Dan, you studmuffin, I want to have your babies!

"Mads!" Lina complained when she read the last line of the proposal Mads had typed up. "Take that out."

"I figured you'd chicken out, so I printed out another copy with no 'p.s.'" She gave Lina the clean copy. "Coward."

"Thank you." Dan was holding office hours that morning to meet with the students about their projects, and Lina had volunteered to present the proposal to him herself.

Dan didn't have an office of his own, so he had to use the *Inchworm* office. *Inchworm*, a student monthly filled with poems and drawings, was one of two literary magazines at Rosewood. The other was the *Rosewood Journal*, which focused on stories, essays, and photography. Lina liked to write, especially poetry, and sometimes thought of joining one of the lit mags. Dan was the faculty advisor for

Inchworm, and Ramona Fernandez was executive editor. Lina knew that was no accident.

Lina sat across the desk from Dan while he read the proposal. She jiggled her right knee nervously. She had never been alone in a room with him before, with the door closed and everything.

Dan was a couple of years out of college, not so much older than Lina really, she thought. He was small and fine-boned, which she found charming, with short brown hair and round blue eyes. Every day he wore vintage suits with narrow lapels and skinny ties. Mads said he looked like Linus from *Peanuts* in a grandpa suit, but Lina liked his style, and she wasn't the only one. Lately Ramona had replaced her usual giant silver cross with a skinny red tie. Talk about super-suck-up. It was supposed to be a symbol of her love for Dan or something. Ramona's friends started doing it, too, but Lina suspected they were just following Ramona. It was turning into a cult thing. The Dan Shulman Cult.

"It's certainly ambitious, Lina," Dan said. "I'll be curious to see if you can really prove your hypothesis."

She strained to think of something cute to say. Why hadn't she planned for this the night before?

"Hey. Speaking of boys versus girls, want to hear a joke?" Dan asked. "I promise it's one hundred percent stupid."

"Sure. I love stupid jokes."

"Okay. An alien walks into a shop and says, 'I'm from Mars and I want to buy a brain for research.' The shop owner shows him three brains. 'This one's a monkey brain,' the shop owner says. 'It costs twenty dollars.' He holds up the second brain and says, 'This is a human female brain, one hundred dollars.' Then he holds up the third brain and says, 'This is a human male brain, five hundred dollars.'

"'Five hundred dollars! Why so expensive?' the alien asks.

"'Well,' the shop owner says, 'it's hardly been used!'"

Lina laughed. "Good one," she said. It wasn't funny but it that made it even cuter.

"I figured I can get away with a self-deprecating joke about my own gender," Dan said.

She wished she could sit there with him all day, casually chatting as if they were comfortable together.

"All right, Lina. Go ahead and post your questionnaire and we'll see what happens! Good luck!"

He smiled at her while she sat frozen in her seat for a second. She knew this was her cue to leave, but her body was a little late in catching on.

"See you in class," Dan added.

Finally her legs straightened and held her weight. "Right. Thanks, Dan."

Holly and Mads were waiting for her in the library. "He likes it," Lina told them. "He says go ahead."

"Great!" Holly said. "I'll post the questionnaire right now."

The three of them had spent several afternoons that week perfecting their questions. Holly opened an account on a Web log site and set up a blog called "The Dating Game." She chose a user name, "hollinmad," and a password for all three girls to use when they logged on.

Holly scanned the quiz onto their blog. A prompt appeared: "Choose a security designation: 1. User Only. 2. Friends Only. 3. Open to All."

"Choose 'Friends only,'" Lina said. "So only people we list as friends can access the site."

"To keep out the hackers," Holly said. "And kids from other schools."

"And parents," Mads added.

"Every entry we make on the blog has its own security setting," Holly said. "So we get to decide which information to keep private and which to share with everybody else."

They pasted in the email addresses of all the students in the school and grouped them as "friends." To log on, the students would have to use their school email addresses.

"So only RSAGE students can read the quiz and answer the questions," Lina said.

"But only we can see their answers," Holly said. "Unless we want to make them public. Then all we have to do is change the security setting."

"I like the part where it says we have 816 'friends,'" Mads said.

Lina took over the keyboard and posted an announcement on the school Web site.

Play the Dating Game! Want to meet a cute guy or girl?
Want to answer some fun quizzes? Want to help us with our
IHD project? It's easy! Log onto the Dating Game Web log and
answer our questionnaire! You must use your RSAGE e-mail
address when you log on. Give your name, your screen name,
or be anonymous, it's up to you. We'll help you find the love
you're looking for. And if you're not in the market for a date,
fill out the questionnaire anyway. It's for a good cause—
helping us get an A in IHD! [Note to juniors and seniors: Come
on, you were in tenth grade once. You took IHD. Have a heart
and help us out! Note to sophomores: We're all in this together!
Note to freshman: This will be you next year!]
                    Holly Anderson, Madison Markowitz, and Lina Ozu

"Now all we have to do is wait for the results," Holly said. "This is kind of exciting!"

"I can't wait to see what people say!" Mads said.

"Be sure to remind everybody about it today," Lina said. "We want to spread the word."

"Got it."

ROSEWOOD SCHOOL FOR ALTERNATIVE GIFTED EDUCATION (RSAGE)

CARLTON BAY, CALIFORNIA

The Dating Game Questionnaire

Boys versus Girls: Who's More Obsessed with Sex?

Please answer all the questions below as completely as possible. As a reward for answering our questions, we will fix you up on a date with another guy or girl who filled out the questionnaire. We will compare your questionnaire with others until we find the person who has what you want, wants what you have, or has the most in common with you. Check the box below if you want to use our matchmaking services.

PART I: TELL US WHO YOU ARE

Screen name:

Gender:

Age:

Grade:

Are you a virgin?

Have you kissed someone of the opposite sex?:

Have you gone to second base? How many times?

Third base? How many times?

Home run? How many times?

How many different people have you had sex with?

Describe your most exciting experience:

Describe your most embarrassing experience:

Describe your scariest experience:

PART II: THE POLL

What's your opinion? Who is more obsessed with sex, boys or girls?

☐ boys ☐ girls

Why?

PART III: THE INKBLOT TEST

Stare at this image. What does it look like to you? Say the first thing that comes into your mind and write it in the space below.

PART IV: MATCH OR NO MATCH?

Do you want us to use this information to match you with someone for a date? Check here. ☐ yes

(When we find someone who seems like a good match, we will e-mail you so you can contact them.)

What are your dating requirements?:

☐ looks ☐ brains ☐ sense of humor ☐ good heart
☐ money ☐ athletic ability ☐ honesty ☐ can carry a
tune other: _____

Dealbreakers? (Please check all that apply.):

☐ bad skin   ☐ meat eater   ☐ vegetarian   ☐ tattoos

☐ piercings   ☐ into fur   ☐ overweight   ☐ underweight

☐ bulimia   ☐ drugs   ☐ drinking   ☐ smoking

other: _____

Thank you for your help. Please check back for updates and results.

"Just think," Mads said. "If Sean fills this out, I can fix myself up on a date with him!"

Lina wished it were that easy for her. She'd ask Dan to fill out the questionnaire for fun, but she knew nothing would come of it. She'd get to him somehow . . . some other way.

4 Fill in the Blanks

HERE IS TODAY'S HOROSCOPE: VIRGO: You will learn some deep truths about your fellow humans. Try not to let it upset you too much.

M ads checked the Web site as soon as she got home from school that afternoon. Thirty kids had already filled out the questionnaire! She couldn't believe it. She quickly typed in the password and started reading. Holly and Lina were IMing her within minutes.

linaonme: Do you believe this? Check out carumba.
mad4u: whoa. He says he lost his virginity in eighth grade!

hollygolitely: juicy7 says she and her boyfriend did it on the
    wrestling mat in the gym.

mad4u: Have you ever done that? had sex at school, I mean.

linaonme: No!

mad4u: Holly?

hollygolitely: Hey, I'm the Boobmeister! Has my rep faded so
    quickly?

Mads couldn't stop reading the questionnaires. She
forgot about her homework, forgot about watching *The
O.C.*, even after her little sister, Audrey, reminded her it
was on. At midnight she brushed her teeth and lay in bed,
staring at the ceiling. She couldn't sleep. She couldn't get
the images of all those kids having all that sex out of her
mind. The voices of the girls talking in the locker room
echoed in her head. How many boys had they seen
naked? How could they be so casual about it?

And meanwhile, what had she done? Kissed a few
boys. Let Toby Buckholtz feel her up at summer camp.
Accidentally saw her older brother, Adam, in the shower
once. And that was about it. She was fifteen years old and
still a virgin. Probably the last virgin left at Rosewood! Or
close to it. It was as if a light went on in her head. Why
didn't she see it before? How could she have let everybody else pass her by this way?

Then there were Lina and Holly. Lina had dated Dmitri

Leshko for about two months last fall. Mads knew something had gone on between them, but she wasn't sure what. Lina could be kind of shy about that stuff. And Holly lost it last summer with that guy in Idaho, Andy. It sounded so beautiful—summer love by a lake, swimming, sailing, sharing ice-cream cones, kissing at sunset, sneaking off together into the woods, snuggling by a campfire . . .

Why hadn't something like that ever happened to her? For Mads, last summer was not what she'd call a sextravaganza. She'd spent most of her time at the pool club, practicing a half-gainer with a twist off the diving board in her pathetic Speedo one-piece. Even eleven-year-old Audrey wore a bikini last summer, but not Mads, oh no. *It might slip off when you're diving.* The little voice in her head mocked her as it spoke these thoughts. Even her own brain was making fun of her.

Was something wrong with her?

Yes. Something was wrong with her. But that was okay, she'd fix it. Things had to change. And fast.

All her life, Mads had been small and cute. People treated her like a little girl. But now she was fifteen, and people still thought of her as a kid. It wasn't the same for Holly, or even Lina. They weren't kids—they were teenagers. Especially Holly. She looked sophisticated, and people believed she was. Why couldn't Mads pull off the same trick?

Mads was afraid of being left behind. Well, it was time to grow up. She was going to catch up with everybody else if it killed her.

I'm going to get some experience, she vowed. She knew exactly whom she wanted to get it with. Another image flashed into her mind. Sean. He shook his hair in the sunlight and smiled his gleaming smile at her. Oh yeah.

She reached for her phone and dialed Holly's cell.

"Hello?" Holly's sleepy voice croaked.

"It's me, Mads. Guess what? I'm going to lose my virginity!"

"That's great, Mads. God, I've got to start turning my ringer off at night."

"And you know who I'm going to lose it with?" Mads said. "Sean Benedetto."

"Good thinking," Holly said. "Choose a guy who's impossible to get. That's a surefire way to lose your virginity."

"What? You don't think I can get him?"

"Well, I didn't say that—"

"Yes you did. You said he was impossible to get. Well, if that's true, how come he's dated six girls since school started this year? Huh? Six! Why shouldn't I be one of them? My turn's got to come sooner or later."

"Well, good luck with that. I've got to go back to sleep now."

Holly was an early-to-bed type, and Mads, a night owl, had no sympathy for her.

"Let's do something tomorrow," Mads said. "I want to plan my complete and utter domination over Sean Benedetto."

But Holly had already hung up.

Holly woke up at eight, the first one up as usual. She padded downstairs in her pajamas and poured herself a cup of coffee. Hooray for automatic coffeemakers. Then she went back to her room, planted her iPod 'phones in her ears, and switched on the computer. What was happening on the Dating Game? Ten more questionnaires had been submitted since the day before. She combed through them. She was supposed to go over to Mads' house, but she knew Mads wouldn't be up for hours.

"Screen name: topgun . . . Age: 16. Grade: 11. Home Run . . . How many times? Over 100. How many different people have you had sex with? I think 37."

Um, okay, sure. That was believable. Next.

She moved on to a girl's questionnaire. "Describe your scariest experience: My scariest experience was when my boyfriend and I were fooling around and the condom broke. I finally got my period two weeks later but the whole two weeks I took a pregnancy test every day even though it was too early to tell."

Wow, Holly thought. *She's only fourteen. That is scary. I didn't realize anyone in our school had already been through something like that.*

She paged through a few questionnaires that seemed honest—guys and girls who admitted to being virgins, who hadn't done much more than kiss, if even that. It helped balance out the wild ones, but she had to admit the truth wasn't as much fun to read.

"Describe your most exciting experience: One time I threw a party but for some reason none of my guy friends showed up. The only people who came were all the cutest girls in school. So we partied by the pool in my backyard and pretty soon all the girls took off their clothes and jumped in . . ."

It got worse from there. Holly checked the age on the questionnaire. *Thirteen? I don't think so. Nice try, Hotpants.*

What was going on here? Were the kids at her school really having as much sex as they said? Holly knew they weren't, no matter what Mads thought. But why were they exaggerating about it—on an anonymous survey?

What if I had to answer these questions? Holly wondered. *What would I say?*

I'd tell the truth, she thought. *Why not? It wasn't so bad.*

Boys had always liked her, even in kindergarten. But in spite of all the rumors, she'd only had sex with one boy, Andy Rufford. Last summer in Idaho.

She'd gone to a lake in Idaho the summer before with her mother and her cousins, who had a house there. Andy was from Seattle. Holly didn't give him much thought at first. He was friends with her cousins, and they all hung out together, and sometimes he was funny. Like the time he put Krazy Glue on the lifeguard's whistle. That was sort of funny.

As the weeks went by, she started to notice that he was cute. Really cute. And he must have noticed her, too, because by August things were heating up between them. Instead of waiting for the rest of the kids, they sneaked out at night to go swimming by themselves. Holly hardly knew how it happened, but soon they were a couple.

They went skinny-dipping. They made out all the time. They moved from second base to third. One night, about a week before the end of the summer, Andy pulled out a condom. He didn't say anything, just showed it to her with a question mark in his eyes. Her heart caught in her throat. This was it. Was she ready? She didn't know, but she decided to go for it.

They fumbled around and it hurt. She had a feeling it was his first time, too, because he didn't seem to know what he was doing. She was so nervous she hardly remembered it, but when it was over she started laughing, and Andy laughed, too. They were like buddies playing a game. That made it less scary.

Later that night she lay in bed alone and thought, *I'm not a virgin anymore.* Was she supposed to feel different somehow? Her heart was beating fast and her face felt hot. But that was about it. She couldn't remember how she'd expected to feel, but she thought it would be a bigger deal than this.

They did it a couple more times. It didn't hurt so much now, and afterward Holly didn't lay awake counting her heartbeats anymore. But there wasn't anything that great about it. Maybe it was because she wasn't deeply in love with Andy. She just liked him a lot. Or maybe they needed more practice to get good at it.

When summer was over, Holly couldn't wait to get home and tell Mads and Lina. But when she tried to explain, she suddenly felt shy. They wanted to know every detail, but she was afraid they wouldn't understand. They seemed to hear the story through a haze of romance. Especially Mads. To her, this was a classic summer love story, and the fact that Holly's first time having sex was awkward, uncomfortable, and not particularly romantic never registered.

Holly scanned the questionnaires again, the answers veering wildly between realistic and raunchy. There had to be somebody datable. She tried to read between the lines. Would a boy called "sexgod" be good for Lina or Mads? Could "zarg" be that cute guy in biology class?

Then she came to "paco." Under "What kind of person are you looking for?" paco wrote, "Madison Markowitz. Period."

Whoa! Who was this guy? Mads had to see this. It was almost noon. Mads should be up by now. Holly couldn't wait to show her paco's questionnaire.

"Good morning, lovey." Holly's mother, Eugenia, sat at the kitchen table in silk pajamas and a robe, drinking coffee while Barbara, the maid, cleared up last night's wine glasses. Eugenia was fine-boned and dark-haired with a raspy smoker's voice, even though she'd quit smoking five years earlier. "Feel like driving up to Petaluma with your sister and me this afternoon? A friend of Piper's has an art show up there. Or something. Maybe it's a performance thing? Whatever."

"No thanks. Busy." Holly fished her car keys out of her bag. "I'm going to Mads' house."

"Be careful on the road," her mother said. "You're still a beginning driver, honey."

Holly had turned sixteen on January 5 and immediately got her driver's license. Her parents gave her a new yellow VW Beetle for her birthday. She loved the car, but sometimes she thought Mads and Lina loved it even more. Lina's birthday wasn't until July 21, and Mads' was even later, August 27. Mads gave Holly driving gloves for her birthday and a map showing the route from Holly's house to hers, even though Holly knew the way cold. Holly was going to be designated chauffeur for a few months. She didn't mind; she already loved driving. And it was way better than depending on her parents or Piper to drive her around, or worse, Mads' older brother Adam, who was 19 and away at college anyway. He had to be the most cautious teenage driver on Earth. Holly's grandma could beat him in a drag race with a blindfold on.

Holly turned a corner and the car climbed Mads' winding, hilly street. Holly felt happy every time she saw the Markowitzes' house. It was built in the seventies and looked like a giant treehouse. Every room seemed to have multiple levels, so that it was hard to tell how many floors the house had. Her mother, M.C., short for Mary Claire, waved to Holly from the organic vegetable garden. She was on her knees, digging, in jeans, a flannel shirt, and red cat's-eye glasses, her frizzy blond hair tied in a red bandanna. She looked like a blond Lucille Ball, just waiting for some hilarious catastrophe to happen.

Mads' parents were warmer than Holly's, and not as slick. Mads thought they were embarrassingly uncool. Her father, Russell, was a good-natured labor lawyer, easily embarrassed and so mild-mannered his children jokingly called him "the Dark Overlord." M.C. met him when she escaped her straight-laced parents' Minnesota farm to go to college at UC Berkeley. She changed careers a lot.

She'd been a yoga teacher, an astrological nutrionist, and the owner of a feminist bookstore. Now she worked as a pet psychiatrist, specializing in troubled dogs. Business was booming; Carlton Bay was a pet-shrink kind of town.

Holly climbed the steep, zigzagging stone steps to the front door. Mads' eleven-year-old sister, Audrey, opened it. She was dressed exactly like a Bratz doll in a midriff-baring t-shirt and low-riding pink sweatpants, her strawberry blond hair scooped high in a side ponytail. Holly didn't know how two down-to-earth people like Russell and M.C. could have such a materialistic super-trendoid for a child.

"Fatison is in her room," Audrey announced, using her favorite nickname for her sister.

When she stepped into Mads' room, Holly was greeted with the rare sight of Mads in glasses. She usually wore contacts. Mads was sitting at her computer, still in her pajamas, reading the questionnaires.

"I'm the biggest loser in school!" Mads wailed. "Have you read these things? Everybody's so experienced! Even the ninth-graders. How did I miss out on this?"

Holly pulled up a chair and sat beside Mads. "You think all these kids are telling the truth? Do you really think three boys in our school have dated *Playboy* centerfolds?"

"I guess that is a little far-fetched," Mads said. "But why would they lie? It's anonymous. Even though I think I can figure out who some of them are by their answers."

"Maybe that's why," Holly said. "Is Lina coming over?"

"Sylvia took her into the city for shopping and lunch," Mads said. Sylvia was Lina's mother. She was a doctor—an allergist—very smart, elegant, and a little chilly. Lina was intimidated by her. She felt closer to her dad, Kenneth, a tall, handsome banker.

"She'll probably come back with another fancy bag to dump in her closet," Holly said. Lina's mother was always buying Lina designer clothes, trying to dress her up.

"It's good that she's not here," Mads said. "Now is the perfect time to match her up with somebody. We've got to get her mind off Dan. She's starting to go all Romeo and Juliet on us. And they both die in the end, you know."

"I'm sure this isn't fatal, but I know what you mean," Holly said. "It doesn't make sense. It's almost like he's brainwashed her or something. Except Dan's too goody-goody to do that."

Holly scanned through the questionnaires and stopped on a junior named "hot-t." "What do you think of this guy for Lina?" she asked Mads.

Mads read it over. "He doesn't sound offensive, at least. But check out this guy." She showed Holly a form by another junior, "striker."

Striker's interests were "soccer, soccer, soccer."

"Striker" was probably a reference to a position on the soccer field.

"I think I know who this is," Holly said. "Jake Soros!"

"Really? Yeah, that kind of makes sense."

Jake Soros, a junior, captain and star of the soccer team. He lived and breathed soccer. Holly suddenly realized that she'd had a crush on him for a long time.

"I want that one for myself," Holly said.

Mads grinned. "Okay. You take striker and we'll sic hot-t on Lina. Cross your fingers that she likes him."

"Now we have to find someone for you," Holly said. "Mads, look at this." She reached around Mads and pulled up paco's form. "You're going to have a stroke." Paco's questionnaire appeared on the screen. "He's totally crazy about you."

Mads read paco's questionnaire carefully. "Who do you think it is?" she asked.

"I have no idea," Holly said.

"Well, one thing's for sure," Mads said. "It's not Sean. Sean's a senior, and paco says he's in eleventh grade."

"So what? You're too good to date juniors now?"

"It's not that," Mads said. "It's just that I want Sean. Do you think he submitted a questionnaire?"

Holly shrugged. "How could we tell?"

"I'll figure it out," Mads said. "If his questionnaire is here, I'll find it."

"But what about paco?" Holly said. "He's in love with you!"

"That's got to be a joke," Mads said. "Wouldn't I know if somebody was in love with me?"

"Maybe he's shy."

"Forget it. Hey, wait a minute. Isn't 'Sean' the same name as 'John,' only Irish? Here's a senior, code name 'john,' who says he looks like Ashton Kutcher except with blond hair! Sean kind of looks like Ashton Kutcher with blond hair!"

Sean didn't look much like Ashton Kutcher, but Holly had to admit that nobody at school looked more like him than Sean.

"Look—he says he wants us to match him with some-body," Mads said. "I volunteer. Let's match him with me!"

"What if it isn't Sean?" Holly asked.

"It's got to be Sean! I'm going to e-mail him right now."

To: john
From: Mad4U
Re: Dating Game
John, you asked us to make a match for you, and we have!
Your date will be a sophomore, 15 years old. If you'd like to meet her, name a time and place and we'll set it up.
Congratulations!

• • •

Five minutes later, an answer appeared.

To: mad4u

From: john

Re: oh yeah

Set it up. How about vineland, after school on Wednesday.
    Cool?

Mad4u: Cool. She'll see you then. How will she know you?

John: just tell her to find the Ashton Kutcher look-alike.

"That was easy," Holly said. "Too easy."

"Stop being so cynical," Mads said. "Isn't that one of the reasons we started this blog? To make getting dates easier? And it's working, see?" She saved the e-mail in a special computer file marked "Sean." "Now we're all taken care of. Let the dating games begin!"

5 Death to the Normals

HERE IS TODAY'S HOROSCOPE: CANCER: Grab your ray gun! An alien life form is about to land on your planet and destroy your life as you know it. This is not a joke.

L ina: You and Holly and Madison have done an excellent job devising a thesis and plan for your project. Go girl! Just be sure to keep careful track of your statistics. I appreciate your offer to let me participate in the study; however, since I'm not a student, I'm afraid my answers would pollute the statistical pool and distort your results. I am looking forward to seeing your first progress report!

Dan ☺

Lina lightly touched the smiley face Dan had made on her paper. Did he put smiley faces on everybody's papers? Only on the good ones? Only on hers? He probably put them on the good ones. He'd left the papers in his outgoing mailbox for all the students to pick up, so anyone could read his comments. Under those circumstances he probably wouldn't put anything personal on a paper. Still, she liked to think there might be a secret message for her hidden somewhere in his comments. "Go girl"? Could that mean something? Besides the fact that he used dated slang? After all, three girls were working on the project, not just one.

She folded up the paper and put it away in her bag. She planned to save it in her keepsake box, along with her dad's school ring, a valentine from a boy she'd liked in first grade, and her "Best Hustle" medal from field hockey, among other exotic memorabilia.

Hockey and Dan were weirdly linked in Lina's mind. She loved playing hockey, loved the way the wooden stick rang in her hand when she smacked the ball just right. She remembered a game near the end of last season, against Rosewood's rival school, Draper. It was a beautiful day and the small bleachers were packed for once, rare for a JV match. Her father had promised to leave work early to catch the game, and she found herself glancing at the bleachers to see if he'd arrived. He hadn't had a chance to see her play all season, but he was her biggest fan, and once in a while he even put on his old lacrosse pads and played goalie against her in the backyard.

During the third quarter she spotted Dan loitering near the sidelines, tie loosened, hands in his pockets, dark sunglasses on, watching, and her heart jammed in her throat. Rebecca passed the ball to her. She gave it a mighty whack and it sailed into the goal. The bleachers went crazy. "Good shot, Lina, good shot," the coach yelled. Lina scanned the crowd for her dad one more time. He wasn't there, but Dan was, clapping and cheering, and it was almost as good.

Two months had gone by, and Lina still thought about that hockey game at least once a day. Now she found herself drifting down the hall past the *Inchworm* office. Through the glass window on the door she could see Dan sitting at a desk, checking proofs.

If she joined *Inchworm*, she'd get to see Dan more. She'd thought about it many times. She loved to write poetry, but she didn't like the poetry *Inchworm* usually published. Most of it was written by Ramona or her friends Siobhan Gallagher, Maggie Schwartzman, and Chandra Bledsoe. All charter members of the Dan Shulman Cult. It was very cryptic, so only they could understand it. There was a lot of blood, death, knives, skulls, and vampire and religious imagery . . . Emily Dickinson meets Night of the

Living Dead. But since they all worked on the magazine, they controlled what was published.

"Excuse me." Ramona and Chandra brushed past her on their way into the office. Ramona's thin red tie was knotted at her throat as usual. Chandra's was black. Those stupid ties! Lina hated the ties. They mocked her. Imitating Dan's dress was no way to pay tribute to his wonderfulness. The best way was Lina's way—silent, painful worship.

"Spying?" Ramona sneered.

Lina was startled. "No! I'm not spying! Why would I be spying?"

Ramona grinned like a jack-o'-lantern. She'd drawn an exaggerated lip line around her real mouth and painted it in with violet lipstick. A little lipstick trickled down from the corner of her mouth, as if she were bleeding, or drooling grape juice.

"We're planning an *Inchworm* reading for next week, if you want to come," Chandra said. She was new to the goth thing and hadn't quite gotten the evil down yet. "We're going to make the office look a like slaughter-house, with blood and body parts everywhere. The theme is 'Death to the Normals.'"

"Oh," Lina said, nodding politely. "Sounds good. I'll tell all my friends."

Ramona heard the sarcasm in Lina's voice. She waited

for Chandra to go into the office. Then she whispered, "I can see it in your eyes, Lina. You think you're better than we are. But you're not. Stop hiding from the truth. You're just like us. Death to the Normals. Don't worry, we'd spare you. You're not normal."

"Great. Thanks." Lina stood frozen in place, watching while Ramona went up to Dan with a sheath of hand-scrawled pages. She knew that was supposed to be a good thing, not being normal. To Ramona, at least.

"I've had a breakthrough," Ramona announced. "My soul has finally reached a higher plane. I stayed up all night documenting it in verse."

"You're so prolific, Ramona," Dan said. "What would *Inchworm* do without you?"

It wouldn't suck, Lina thought.

Why did she care what Ramona and her friends did? It had nothing to do with her. But it upset her. Everything about them. Especially the ties.

She was a normal, popular girl, right? Well, popular-ish. She and Holly and Mads were friendly with the cool kids but they weren't indisputably the cool kids themselves, not yet anyway. But Lina wasn't like those fringe-dwellers. She didn't pierce weird parts of her body or dye every-thing dyable or worship some made-up goddess of death.

But she did love Dan. And so did they. Deep down, maybe she was more like them than she wanted to admit.

6 Mr. Yuck

HERE IS TODAY'S HOROSCOPE: VIRGO: Someone is broadcasting geek rays—and you're receiving them loud and clear.

Mads scanned the parking lot at Vineland for Sean's car. He drove a Jeep. No sign of it. He must not be here yet.

She waved to Holly and Lina, who'd dropped her off. They waved back and drove off to wait out the date at Holly's. Mads walked into the café and looked around. No Sean, and no one else who looked like a blond Ashton Kutcher, either. Mads went to the bathroom to check her hair, makeup, and clothes. This was the most important day of her life. Her first date with Sean!

Holly and Lina had helped her get ready. Mads insisted she wanted smoky eye makeup for the mysterious look she believed appropriate for a blind date, even a blind date that took place at four in the afternoon. So Lina smudged black eyeliner around her eyes and Mads wouldn't let her stop until she looked like someone had punched her. Holly was in charge of the red lipstick.

Mads studied the results in the bathroom mirror at Vineland. She wasn't sure how she looked, but one thing she knew, and liked, was that she didn't look like her usual self. As far as she was concerned, that was an improvement.

She wanted to look sexy but she didn't want to over-dress. The eternal problem. So she wore fishnet stockings under her short corduroy skirt instead of her usual tights, and high-heeled boots. She left her black hair hanging down naturally.

She went back into the café and picked out a table. It was four o'clock exactly. She grabbed a magazine and flipped through it, trying to look casual. Ten minutes went by, fifteen. Where was Sean?

At 4:17, the door opened and a gangly, pallid boy with giant feet and a brown pageboy haircut walked in, flourishing a red satin cape. Mads recognized him. He was a ninth-grader known as Yucky Gilbert. His real name was Gilbert Marshall, and he was supposed to be super-smart. He'd skipped two grades and was only twelve. People called him Yucky because he was beyond dorky, snorted when he laughed, and ate things like peanut-butter-and anchovy-sandwiches for lunch. You could tell because he often had a bit of anchovy paste stuck to the side of his mouth at the end of the day.

Mads went back to her magazine, but a shadow fell across the page. She looked up. Gilbert, who was tall for his age but skinny, loomed over her.

"Hello, Madison," Gilbert crooned.

"Hello." Mads went back to her magazine.

"May I sit down?"

"No. I'm waiting for someone."

"I know." Mads looked up. How could he know?

"You're waiting for me," Yucky Gilbert said. "I'm 'john.'"

Mads swallowed. She felt lightheaded.

"You're john? But you can't be! John looks like Ashton Kutcher! He's a junior!"

Gilbert flipped his cape and sat down across from her. "Sorry. I lied."

"You lied! That's not allowed! How can you be matched up with the right person if you lie on your questionnaire?" Mads was furious.

"What's a little lie when the love of your life is at stake?"

"The love of your life?" Mads stared at him, not understanding. She still couldn't accept that Sean Benedetto wasn't going to show up.

Gilbert reached for her hand. She snatched it away.

"Madison Markowitz, you are the prettiest girl in the whole school. The town. The state of California. The good old U.S. of A. The Western Hemisphere. The—"

"Stop! I get it," Mads snapped.

"The universe," Gilbert finished. "And I'm gazoygle about you."

Mads squinted at him. "Gazoygle? What does that mean?"

"It's Blastoph—a special alien language I made up myself. It means I'm crazy about you."

"Does your special alien language have a word for 'Get lost'?" Mads asked. "Or 'Leave me alone'?"

"Of course," Gilbert said. "But those are phrases, not words." He reached for her hand again. Mads sat on both her hands to keep them from veering into his air space.

"I understand—this is a big surprise," Gilbert said. "I'll go to the counter and get us something. What would you like? They have cupcakes with jelly beans on them."

"I would like you to go away," Mads said. "I'm not having a date with you."

"You have to," Gilbert said. "You fixed yourself up with me. And anyway, what about your project? You have to report on our date."

"Who says? You lied on your form, so it doesn't count." Mads' eyes frantically darted around the room.

Who was there? Who saw her talking to Gilbert? Sitting at a table with him? On a date with him!

This was exactly the opposite of what Mads was hoping to accomplish. She wanted experience. She wanted a more mature image. She wanted Sean. She was not going to get any of those things from dating a geeky twelve-year-old. Just being seen with him would nuke her rep back to the Stone Age.

"You—you made yourself sound like a totally different person," Mads said. "How could you do that?"

"I used Sean Benedetto as a model," Gilbert admitted. "I mean, why not? Girls like him. It seemed like the best way to get a date."

"It's wrong!" Mads said. She got up from the table before someone she knew walked in and spotted her. "And I won't go on a date with a liar! Under false pretenses! Et cetera!"

She stormed out of the café, tripping over a rug in her high heels. She could call her mother to come pick her up, but she didn't want to wait, and her house wasn't too far away. So she walked all the way home in her heels, tears and black makeup streaming down her cheeks.

> mad4U: total disaster! my date wasn't sean. who do you think
> it was? imagine the worst person possible.
> linaonme: hitler?

mad4U: no, doofus, someone who goes to rosewood. yucky
gilbert!

mad4U: hollygolitely???

hollygolitely: oh my god.

mad4U: he totally lied. i stormed out of there and walked
home and now i have a wicked blister on my heel.

linaonme: I hope our dates don't turn out like that.

mad4u: thanx a lot.

linaome: if they suck I'm blaming you, holly.

hollygolitely: I can't guarantee another gilbert won't show up.
But I've done my best to weed out the dregs. I try to
give you the finest service for your matchmaking dollar.

linaonme: maybe we'd better double. That way, at least we'll
suffer together. I mean, I know you think jake soros is
going to show up but mads' sad story proves that you
never know. If your date turns out to be a lying geek
you'll be glad I'm there.

hollygolitely: ok. We'll double for the first date.

mad4u: I hate being the guinea pig.

linaonme: maybe there's a way we can weed out the geeks.

mad4u: a geek quiz. I think I have enough experience in this
area to work up a few questions. It probably won't weed
them out but we could post it on our site as a public
service, so geeks can identify themselves and get help.

hollygolitely: go to it.

Quiz: Are You a Geek?

We suspect that you know who you are. But if there's any question,
take this quiz and find out your true geek status.

1. **The first thing you do when you wake up in the morning is:**

   a ▶ Brush your teeth

   b ▶ Check your e-mail

   c ▶ Dig into a 3-day-old pizza you found under your bed

   d ▶ Step on your glasses by accident, then try to fix them with
   black electrical tape

2. **When getting dressed for school, you:**

   a ▶ Call your friends to see what they're wearing

   b ▶ Put on the carefully chosen outfit you laid out the night
   before

   c ▶ Put on the first thing you trip over on the floor

   d ▶ Dust off your Star Trek costume

3. **The first thing people notice about you is:**

   a ▶ Your bright smile

   b ▶ Your fashion sense

   c ▶ Your odd haircut

   d ▶ A funny smell

4. **Your favorite subject in school is:**

   a ▶ Gym

   b ▶ English

c ▶ Science

d ▶ Math

5. Your idea of the perfect evening is:

    a ▶ Dinner and a movie with someone cute

    b ▶ Hanging with your friends

    c ▶ Doing a jigsaw puzzle with your mother

    d ▶ You, your computer, and a box of Hostess cupcakes

6. When you grow up, you want to be:

    a ▶ A movie star

    b ▶ A doctor

    c ▶ A computer-game inventor

    d ▶ Frodo

Scoring: mostly a's: Geek-Free

mostly b's: Touch O' Geek

mostly c's: Major Geek Tendencies

mostly d's: Total Geekosity

I hope every geek at RSAGE takes this quiz and reforms, Mads thought. Assuming reform was possible. Mads couldn't imagine the treatment required to make Gilbert geek-free. But that wasn't her problem anymore. All she knew was she never wanted to go on another date like that again.

7 Prove That You're a Human

HERE IS TODAY'S HOROSCOPE: CANCER: You're oh-so-sensitive and often think your friends don't understand you. But maybe they <u>do</u> understand you. Maybe you <u>are</u> crazy. Feel better now?

I'm so glad we decided to do this together. I could never go through with it by myself," Lina said.

Holly parked in front of Zola's, a bustling seafood cafe near the Carlton Bay Marina. It was Saturday night, time to find out the true identities of "striker" and "hot-t." She stared through the restaurant windows as if they'd offer her a clue.

"Sure you could," Holly said. "You just didn't want to."

That was true. Lina didn't know who hot-t was, but the one thing she did know about him—that he wasn't Dan—left her pretty much not interested.

Holly reached for the door, but Lina grabbed her arm. "Let's make a pact," Lina said. "If one of us is unhappy and wants to leave, we'll say, 'I've got a terrible headache.'"

"That sounds too fake," Holly said.

"How about I take my cell phone out and say 'Mom is text-messaging me that the house just blew up and I have to go home right away'?"

"Too dramatic," Holly said. "Why don't we just say we're getting a call and we have to take it? Then the miserable girl—and it already looks like it's going to be you, from your bad attitude—steps away and the other girl goes to see what's wrong and we tell the boys there's some kind of family crisis. Okay?"

"Okay." She took a deep breath and opened the door. "Let's go."

They walked into the cafe. Holly spotted Jake right away—stocky, muscular, black hair trimmed close to his rather big head—sitting at the counter with a familiar-looking guy. "That must be them," she said.

She led the way, Lina following. Lina tried to get a handle on her date. He swiveled around in his seat as they approached. He was taller than she was—good start. Maybe a little too thin. Medium-brown dreadlocks cinched in a neat knot behind his head, tied with a red cord. Pale-brown skin, almost beige, and green eyes. She had to admit he was pretty cute.

"Which one of you is striker?" Holly asked.

Jake waved. "I am. My real name is Jake Soros." As if she didn't know. He nodded at the guy next to him. "I recognized this dude from school. Turns out he's meeting a blind date, too."

"That's me," Lina said. "Lina Ozu."

"I'm Walker Moore," Lina's date said. Walker Moore—the name sounded familiar. She'd seen him around school of course, but there was something else. . . .

"And I'm Holly Anderson." They sounded like a bunch of news anchors soberly identifying themselves.

Jake stood up and said, "Let's get a table."

Holly followed Jake to a corner table. The cafe bustled. Holly felt excited. She'd been to parties and dances with boys, had meals with them, but hadn't been on a lot of real, honest-to-god dates. This felt like a real date.

They sat down, and Lina realized how she knew Walker's name. "Hey," she asked. "Do you write for the *Seer*?" The Rosewood *Seer* was the school's student newspaper.

"Sports," he said. "That's how I know Jake." Jake, star of the soccer team, was regularly featured on the *Seer*'s sports page.

Lina liked that Walker wrote for the paper. But she still couldn't help wondering, if he was such a great guy, why did he choose "hot-t" for a screen name? It seemed kind of conceited.

A waiter arrived to take their orders. The menu was printed on the paper placemats. "I tried to order a beer at the counter but they wouldn't serve me," Jake said after the waiter left.

"We can get some after dinner if we feel like it," Walker said. "I've got a fridge-full at my house."

After dinner? Just how long was this date going to last? Lina wondered.

"So, you write about sports?" Holly asked. "Lina writes, too."

"That's cool," Walker said. "What do you write?"

"Mostly poetry and stories and stuff," Lina said.

"I hate to write," Jake said. "It was all I could do just to check the boxes on that dating quiz you made up."

"Did you like the quiz?" Holly asked.

"Yeah, it was fun," Jake said. "RSAGE is a pretty big school. There are lots of cute girls I never met before." He grinned at Holly and tapped her foot with his under the table.

Holly felt warm. He liked her! She'd watched him play every home game this year and last. Maybe he didn't look like much just sitting across the table from her—although he *was* cute, with his black fuzz for hair and even some stubble on his chin. Manly. He seemed older than his years. You could see it on the field, with his powerfully-built body and amazing speed. He was captain. The team followed him, and he really led them. Something about that got to Holly.

"You guys should have made the championships last year," Walker said. "Mill Valley was fouling all over the place and the refs never called it!"

"Tell me about it," Jake said. "Those refs all live in Mill Valley. I think we'll make it next year, though. The freshman squad has some good guys coming up."

The food smelled good: fried fish sandwiches and steaming bowls of chowder. Jake smiled at Holly and tapped her foot under the table again. They all started eating. The table was silent until Jake said to Walker, "Have you seen this guy Freddy Adu play soccer? He's our age and he's already a pro . . ."

Holly glanced at Lina. They sat quietly listening until they got bored. It looked as if the soccer conversation was not ending anytime soon. So they entertained themselves by analyzing the latest posting on "Nuclear Autumn." Apparently Autumn's dad was dating a twenty-four-year-old and Autumn was planning to sabotage it.

I should never have let Lina talk me into double-dating, Holly thought. The boys were paying more attention to each other than to the girls.

The check came and the boys paid it. Lina and Holly offered to split it but the boys refused. Finally they were acting as if they were on a date.

"What do you guys want to do now?" Jake asked. "It's still early."

"Why don't we go hang at my house?" Walker asked. "My mom's cool and we'll have the garage to ourselves."

Maybe things will pick up at Walker's house, Holly thought. Sometimes boys didn't feel comfortable in restaurants—all that sitting in chairs and keeping their shirts tucked in was hard for them. But they'd relax at Walker's. And who knew where things could go from there?

Lina pulled her cell phone out of her purse. "It's on vibrate," she lied, glancing at the screen as if to see who was calling. "Oh god, my mom's texting me. Our house exploded!"

"What?" Walker cried.

"She's just joking," Holly said, and Lina threw her a dirty look.

"Whoa!" Lina cried, staring at the screen. "My parents are being held hostage by a crazed gunman! I'd better get home!"

"Ha ha," Holly said. "Isn't she hilarious?"

Lina frowned. "But seriously, my mom is calling, and she wouldn't call if it wasn't important," she said, getting up from her chair. "I'll just go take this over there." She walked toward the bathroom.

"I'll be right back," Holly said, following her.

"What's with you?" Holly asked as Lina stuffed her phone back into her purse.

"Do you really want to go to Walker's house?" Lina asked. "I'd like to cut things short tonight."

"Come on, Lina, don't punk out on me," Holly said.

"Walker's okay but I'm just not clicking with him."

"You're not trying," Holly said. "Jake keeps playing footsie with me under the table. Please, Lina. I just want to see where things go with him tonight. He's so . . . powerful."

Lina rolled her eyes. "What am I going to do while you guys are playing footsie?"

"Talk to Walker! He's a nice guy. And he writes!"

"About sports. Not really my thing. Except for field hockey. Which he probably doesn't even care about."

"Maybe he has a secret sensitive side you can discover at his house. I'm sure he does! All boys have them."

"How do you know?"

"I read it in *Seventeen*. Which, as Mads will tell you, is the source of all truth. Please, Lina? Do this for me? Just this once?"

"All right. I'm only doing it for you. This once."

"Thank you, thank you! I owe you one."

The boys stood by the front door, waiting for them.

"All set?" Jake asked. "So, you want to go over to Walker's?"

"Sounds great," Holly said. "I'll follow you in my car."

Walker lived a couple of miles away in a modern hillside house. Walker's mom greeted them in the kitchen in her bathrobe, ready for bed.

"If you need anything, just rummage around," she said. "The kitchen's pretty well-stocked. Well, good-night, honey." She squeezed Walker's cheeks together with one hand and kissed him. He made a face but underneath the smirk was a smile. "Don't stay up too late. And don't wake your brothers."

"We won't," Walker promised.

"Wow, your mom goes to bed early," Jake said. It was 9:30.

"Yeah. She has to get up early for work," Walker said.

He grabbed a bowl of chips and led the way to a garage that had been converted to a rec room. "There's another fridge in there where Mom keeps all the beer," he said.

The garage was carpeted and had a big leather couch, a loveseat, a flat-screen TV, a great sound system, remote-control lighting, and a bar. Holly sat down on the loveseat. Lina plopped down beside her. Holly gave her a dirty look, but Jake saved the day. "Why don't you sit over here next to me, Holly?" he asked, patting the empty spot beside him on the couch.

Holly moved over to the couch. She was nervous. Did he really like her? After all, *he* hadn't asked her out. She'd fixed herself up with him. And a little voice in the back of her mind said, *What if? What if to him you're just Boobmeister Holly, the girl with the supertits who bagged Nick Henin?* Stupid voice. She squelched it. Those little voices weren't always right, anyway.

Walker put on some music and opened a beer for each of them. Holly sipped hers, grateful for something to do with her hands. Lina put hers down on the coffee table, untouched.

"Don't you like beer?" Walker asked. "We've got wine, too, or vodka and stuff if you want."

"That's okay," Lina said. "I like beer. I'm just not in a beery mood right now."

She hated the sound of her own voice as she heard it speak the words. Why was she being such a priss? She wasn't always like this with boys, but that night it was as if her body was possessed by the chilly spirit of her mother. Lina had always vowed not to be like her mother, but here she was, snippily refusing drinks and spoiling everyone's night.

What was Lina's problem? Holly wondered. She was acting like Princess Buzzkill. Walker was cute and nice . . . just because he wasn't their damn teacher . . .

Walker dimmed the lights and sat beside Lina on the

loveseat. The music was loud, thank god, Lina thought. Because she had no idea what to talk about. And nobody else seemed to, either. It was a little awkward. Holly crossed her legs and bounced her foot to the beat of the music.

Jake did the whole yawn-and-put-your-arm-around-the-girl thing. Holly smiled. "Like that move?" he asked.

"Smooth," she said.

He pulled her close and kissed her on the lips a little tentatively, as if he couldn't quite remember how that kissing thing worked. Holly was surprised. Jake looked like a take-charge kind of guy when it came to girls. But who knew? Maybe this was a tactic to put her off-guard. Anyway it was a start. Holly wished she could have brushed her teeth after dinner. She could still taste the clam chowder on her tongue. Ick.

Just go for it, she told herself. She kissed him back shyly. The stubble around his mouth felt rough. Holly had never kissed a guy with so much beard before.

He pulled back, looked in her eyes, then dove in for more. His kiss was more forceful now but still seemed a little iffy. She kissed him back, felt herself loosening up a little, and opened her mouth. He didn't respond, so she darted her tongue into his mouth.

She vaguely sensed a tangle of limbs across the room and thought, *Good for Lina*.

Holly and Jake were off in their own world. Walker

stroked Lina's hair while she struggled to think of something to say. If only she liked boy sports! That seemed an endless source of foolproof boy talk. She vowed to watch more baseball this year.

"You have nice hair," Walker said. "It's so shiny."

"Thanks," Lina said.

"Do you put something special in it? To make it so smooth, I mean?"

"Baby oil," Lina replied.

"Me, too," Walker said. "Only it doesn't seem to work for me."

This had to be a low point in the history of date conversation.

They both found their eyes trailing over toward Holly and Jake grappling on the couch. From where they were sitting it looked pretty intense.

Walker's hand moved from Lina's hair to the sleeve of her blouse. Lina stiffened. Just because Holly and Jake were going at it, she and Walker had to, too? She hardly knew the guy!

Walker suddenly pulled her body against his and pressed her head to his chest. "Your hair smells so good." What was it with this guy and hair? He rubbed the back of her blouse. Lina had the feeling he was groping for a way under it.

Lina pressed him away with both hands. "Walker—"

He immediately let her go. "I'm sorry, I'm sorry," he said.

"No, it's okay," Lina said, feeling badly now. She didn't want to hurt his feelings. "It's just, well, I'd like to get to know you better before we get into the whole makeout scene."

"I get you," Walker said. "No problem." He glanced across the room at Jake and Holly again. They were in their own world.

"Do you think they'd mind if I turned on the TV?" Walker whispered to Lina.

"I don't think they'll even notice," Lina said.

Jake was kissing Holly more feverishly now, getting into it. Holly began to lose herself in it, a kind of makeout amnesia. He slipped his hand under her sweater, touching the bare skin on her back. She pressed herself against him, excited.

And then he froze. His lips went slack, his hand dropped out of her sweater, and he pulled away.

What did she do wrong?

"Jake?" she whispered. "You okay?"

"Sure," he said, disentangling himself from her. "Everything's cool. I just thought I'd get another beer. You want one?"

Holly watched in disbelief as he stood and went to the bar fridge. He glanced back at her, repeating his question with his eyes. Another beer?

"No thanks," she said. "I've still got some." She picked up her bottle, warm now, and took a tepid sip. The TV was on. Lina and Walker were sitting on the loveseat, not touching, watching a Japanese cartoon.

Jake returned with his beer. He sat on the other side of her, at the end of the couch, one whole leather cushion away.

What just happened? Holly wondered. He'd pulled away when she pressed herself against him. Did she come on too strong?

Jake turned his head and smiled at her, then turned back to the cartoon. That was it. Holly didn't feel like sticking around.

"Hey, Lina, I guess we should get going soon," she said.

Lina practically leaped to her feet. "Yeah, my parents are waiting up."

"Oh, you have to go?" Walker seemed disappointed.

"Yeah, you know, eleven o'clock curfew," Holly said. She had no such thing—her parents were pretty lax—but Jake didn't need to know that.

The boys stood up and walked them to the front door. "See you again soon, Lina," Walker said.

"'Bye," Lina said.

"I'll walk you to your car," Jake said.

Lina and Holly walked to Holly's Beetle, trailed by Jake. Lina got into the passenger seat. Holly leaned against the driver-side door. Jake kissed her lightly and said, "It was great to meet you. I'll call you soon."

"Great," Holly said. She opened the door and got in. "Thanks for dinner! Bye!"

She pulled out of the driveway. "Where to?" Lina asked. "I don't feel like going home yet."

"Me neither," Holly said. "The Markowitz Mansion?"

"Perfect."

"I don't get it, Lina," Mads said. She sat cross-legged on her Indian-print bedspread. "What, he wasn't cute?"

"He was cute," Holly said.

"He was cute," Lina repeated. "So what? Captain Meow-Meow is cute, too, but you don't make out with him." She picked up Mads' persnickety Siamese cat and gave him a squeeze. He jumped out of her arms and ran away.

"Don't take it personally," Mads said. "Mom says Captain Meow-Meow's been having boundary issues ever since we adopted Boris."

Boris was the Markowitzes' new boxer puppy. He was downstairs in the living room being trained by M.C., whose idea of pet discipline involved a lot of candles and chanting. Audrey and Russell were playing a video game

79

together. All this at eleven o'clock at night, when Lina's house would have been dark and quiet, just a light on in her room and one in her parents', where they would be in bed reading. This was why Lina loved Mads' house—24-hour chaos.

"What about Holly?" Lina said to Mads. "Why don't you pick on her for a while?"

"Hey, I tried," Holly said. "Jake didn't come through."

"Maybe he wants to take things slowly," Mads said. "He must really like you if he doesn't want to rush things."

"I don't know," Holly said. "What if he just didn't like me? What if he thinks I'm hideous? What if he thought I had bad breath? Maybe he hates the taste of chowder."

"He had chowder, too," Lina reminded her. "He probably couldn't even taste it on you."

"And you're beautiful, so how could he think you're hideous?" Mads added. "Don't panic. Wait and see if he calls you. I think he's just not a player. Which is a good thing."

"I hope you're right," Holly said. "But that's not the vibe I'm getting."

Mads looked from Holly to Lina and back again. One liked her guy, but he was acting weird. The other didn't like her guy, even though he clearly liked her. Was love always this way?

"Well, at least it sounds like Walker likes you, Lina,"

Mads said. "All that talk about your shiny, good-smelling hair."

"He does like her," Holly said. "And he seems really cool. Lina just wouldn't give him a chance."

"That's not true," Lina protested. "I like him okay. There's nothing wrong with him or anything. We just didn't click, that's all."

"Is it because of Dan?" Mads asked. "If it is, you're a moron."

"No," Lina lied. "It's not Dan."

She was too embarrassed to admit the truth. She didn't just *like* Dan. She was crazy about him! She thought about him constantly. She could never like another guy, ever. Ever. How could a high school guy compare? They were so boring. And silly. All that talk of sports and shiny hair. Where was the poetry? The passion?

Holly and Mads would never understand. They liked regular boys. That was fine with Lina. If they could be satisfied with subhumans, good for them.

8 The Social Goddesses

Class: Interpersonal Human Development
Teacher: Dan Shulman
The Dating Game: Progress report: Week 1
By Holly Anderson, Madison Markowitz, and Lina Ozu

The Dating Game Web site received an enthusiastic response from the data pool—that is, the students at RSAGE. At the time of this report, out of 816 students, 207, or more than one-quarter, have filled out the questionnaire. Of the respondents, about 65 percent are female and 35 percent are male.

As for our thesis (who's more sex-crazed, boys or girls?), results so far indicate a tie. However, our statistical pool is lop-sided. We need more answers from boys. We feel confident that with further study, our hypothesis, that boys are more sex-crazed, will be confirmed.

The results of the questionnaires are compiled on the charts and graphs attached. We posted these charts on the site so the students can see how their answers compare with the other students'. As you can see, many students claim to have extensive sexual experience. If some of this is an exaggeration, we cannot be held responsible.

As for matchmaking, so far we have sent ten couples on dates. Two were successful (we define success as both parties agreeing to a second date). Two were complete disasters. The jury is still out on the rest of them.

The Dating Game, Questionnaire #2:
Who's More Sex-Crazed, Boys or Girls?

All right, people. Let's try this again. And if you are a boy, please respond. We need more answers from boys.

Do You Have Sex on the Brain?
Check the box next to each statement that is true for you.
1. ☐ I am a boy
2. ☐ I am a girl

3. ☐ I dreamed about sex last night

4. ☐ I dream about sex every night

5. ☐ I think soap operas are sexy

6. ☐ I think *The Price Is Right* is sexy

7. ☐ My parents never knock before coming into my room, and I have no problem with that

8. ☐ My best friend is of the opposite sex. If he/she fell in love with me, I'd freak out

9. ☐ My best friend is of the opposite sex. If he/she fell in love with me, I'd be thrilled

10. ☐ I watch <u>MTV Spring Break</u> for the travel tips

11. ☐ When I say someone is cute, I mean it in a stuffed-animal kind of way

12. ☐ When I say someone is cute, it means I'm picturing him/her naked

Answer Key: If you checked boxes 7, 8, 10, and 11 you're a prude. If you checked boxes 3, 5, and 9, you're fairly normal. If you checked boxes 4, 6, and 12, you're a total perv.

"Well, if it isn't the Boobmeister," Sebastiano purred. "Looks like you just took a step up on the social ladder, Holly. I'll have to try to be seen in public with you more often."

Monday morning and the halls were buzzing with talk of the Dating Game. Holly had picked up on it, too, but her twice-daily meeting with Sebastiano at their lockers kept her up to date on the very latest.

"I heard that Ingrid found some kind of love slave on your Web site," Sebastiano said. "The guy actually came to her house and cleaned her room for her! He even shined her shoes! She's in heaven!"

"Good morning, Sebastiano," Holly said, as if he were a normal person who had normal conversations. "How was your weekend?"

"I love those charts you guys made," Sebastiano said. "Showing how experienced the student body is. I had no idea this school was so full of perverts!" He glanced around, as if the dorky boy walking by with his skateboard could be a secret sex fiend. "It's very exciting. It changes the whole concept of school! Like, what will we be learning today?"

Holly pawed through a pile of books on her locker shelf. "Do we have a quiz in Geometry today?"

"Do we? Oh no! I didn't study. Did you ask about my weekend? It's all hazy now. Must have been good."

"Sounds better than mine," Holly said.

"Better than yours? How can that be? Your weekend was spent luxuriating in the creation of the greatest invention to hit Rosewood since girls' volleyball. A sex Web site! Detailing the innermost thoughts and desires of every punk in school! Pure genius." He kissed his fingertips, Italian-style. He could be a real ham, that Sebastiano. "You were basking in your triumph! Weren't you?"

"I didn't do much basking," Holly said, though it was beginning to dawn on her that maybe she should.

"Hmm. According to 'Nuclear Autumn' you've been seeing a lot of action."

"You can't believe everything you read," Holly said. "Autumn doesn't have the guts to write about my *real* activities."

"Ooh. Tell me. I can take it. I'm unshockable."

Holly was bluffing, of course, but she wasn't exactly lying. Autumn *wouldn't* want to write about her date with Jake. It was too boring.

But Holly had seen all the talk about her on the Web. A wallful of virtual graffiti about "the Boobmeister." Anonymous chatters told stories of spotting Holly naked with Nick at the Christmas party; Holly going around grabbing guys' crotches; Holly standing on the corner of Rutgers and Tapp Streets, dressed like a hooker. . . . She tried not to let it bother her, but it pissed her off. How could people just make up stuff like that?

And here was Sebastiano, practically drooling as he waited to hear about her thrilling weekend. She hated to let him down.

"I'll spare you the details. Let's just say I went on a blind date."

"Don't spare the details! That's the best part!"

"Sorry. I don't kiss and tell."

"Just tell me who he is," Sebastiano pleaded.

She hesitated. She'd known Sebastiano since sixth grade, but he wasn't really a friend. They never talked on the phone or IM'ed each other or went out of their way to get together outside of school. But through alphabetical coincidence, their lockers had been side-by-side for five years now. They were seated together at every assembly. They were close acquaintances. And in his odd way he was usually honest with her. "Jake Soros."

"That soccer hooligan? Holly, you can do better. He could use some manscaping. Though he is built."

"Manscaping?"

"You know, grooming: Clean the nails, shave a little closer—he's a pretty hairy dude. He's going to have a wicked back hair problem when he grows up."

Holly hadn't noticed anything other than the chin stubble. Maybe he'd cleaned his nails for their date. "I like him," she said.

"You have lousy taste," he said.

"How would you know?"

"I see what goes on around this dump. I know all."

"Well, who do you think is hot?"

"I'll take my cue from you and spare you 'the details.' That'll teach you to be discreet. Later." He shut his locker and started down the hall.

"I'm not letting you cheat off me in Geometry!"

He spun around and shook his finger at her. "You'll do as I say!" A couple of guys snickered as they walked by. Lina and Mads, clutching their books, came up and said hello to Sebastiano.

"Hello, girls," he said. "How are you enjoying your new status as social goddesses?"

"Social goddesses?" Mads beamed. "When did that happen?"

"Overnight!" Sebastiano called as he disappeared around a corner. "These things always happen overnight."

"What was that all about?" Lina asked.

"Just a little trip to Planet Sebastiano," Holly said.

"I do think more people said hi to me than usual this morning," Mads said.

The first warning bell rang. Holly closed her locker. "Let's get some coffee before class."

They headed for the lunch room, where coffee, tea, and bagels could be bought any time before lunch. Rebecca Hulse stood by the cash register, adding milk to her coffee.

"Hey, chickies," she called to Holly, Lina, and Mads.

"Hi, Beck," Lina said.

"I'm having a party this weekend," Rebecca said. "Saturday night. Nothing big, but you guys should definitely come. A few of your Dating Game hookups will be there—you can see how it all plays out."

"Cool," Holly said, surprised that Rebecca was bothering to invite them to a party. Not that she'd ever purposely exclude them. It just wasn't like her to go out of her way to *include* them.

"Yeah, our research requires constant party-going," Mads said. "It's a tough job, but somebody's got to do it."

"You know, I submitted a questionnaire on your site, but you haven't matched me up with anybody," Rebecca said. "When are you going to get to me?"

"Sorry—it takes time to do it right," Lina said. "We'll get to you soon."

"Good," Rebecca said. "I want a slave boy, like Ingrid got. My room is a mess." She left. Holly, Lina, and Mads perched at a table for the few minutes left before Modern World History.

"Hmm. It seems like our matchmaking skills work for everybody except us," Holly said. "I haven't heard a peep from Jake. Has Walker called you, Lina?"

"Last night," Lina admitted.

"Why didn't you tell us?" Mads said.

Lina shrugged. "It's no big deal. He wanted to get together this weekend."

"Wow, he called you the next day," Mads said. "He must really like you. What are you guys going to do?"

"Nothing," Lina said. "I told him I was busy."

"What? But you're not busy!" Mads said.

Lina knew they wouldn't understand. "I'm just not

feeling it. Why should I force myself to go out with him if I know he's not It?"

"Because you don't know he's not It," Holly said. "You haven't given him a chance."

"I do know."

"How did he take it?" Mads asked. "Being rejected, I mean."

"He was pretty cool about it," Lina said.

Holly felt a tiny nip of jealousy. Why hadn't Jake called her yet? What good was popularity if everybody liked her except *him*?

9 Current Mood: About to Burst

To:	mad4u
From:	Your daily horoscope

HERE IS TODAY'S HOROSCOPE: VIRGO: Do you believe in miracles? I hope so, because your losing streak is coming to an end. Enjoy it while it lasts.

Four hours later, Mads sat at the middle table in the lunch room, waiting for Lina and Holly. Sean and two of his friends, Alex Sipress and Mo Basri, came in and sat at the table next to Mads. She immediately lost her appetite.

"Dudes, why didn't you go to Superscope Saturday night?" Sean said. "Boardman and I ran into these college chicks. They were *so hot*. They were post-apocalyptic."

"What are you, trying to sound smart for the college

girls?" Alex said. "Save yourself five syllables and just say they were hot."

Mads smiled. Post-apocalyptic. She liked it. But it sounded familiar. She's seen it or heard it somewhere recently, exactly the way Sean used it. But where?

Holly sat down. "You know, I love Geometry," Holly said. "I think I aced the quiz today—"

"That's it!" Mads jumped to her feet. That was where she'd seen the word—on one of the questionnaires. And there was an excellent chance that whoever wrote "post-apocalyptic" on his questionnaire was Sean. She hadn't heard anyone else use the word that way, though she was expecting it to go wide any day now.

"I'm going to the library," Mads said. "Back later."

She hurried to the library and commandeered one of the computers. She scanned the boys' questionnaires until she found it: "I like all kinds of girls, but especially girls who really knock me over, who are like, so hot they're post-apocalyptic."

Name of the boy: "p_diddy." Of course. Like Sean "P. Diddy" Combs. Sean! It had to be Sean!

Mads had him now. This time he wouldn't get away.

> mad4u: u set it up, holly. I don't want him to think I'm chasing
>   him. I want him to think that you compared our question-
>   naires and decided that the best girl in the whole school

for him is me. Based on totally scientific evidence and
all that.

hollygolitely: ok. I'll tell him to email you to set up a date.

mad4u: thanks, h. I hope he writes right away. I'm so excited!

Mads signed off and tried to do her homework.
Downstairs a dog howled pitifully. M.C. was seeing one of
her patients, a Doberman with separation anxiety.

Mads did her Spanish homework, then checked her
e-mail. Nothing. She IM'ed Holly.

mad4u: did you e-mail him yet?

hollygolitely: yes, an hour ago. Relax, he might not even read
it till later.

Mads tried reading her history textbook. It was
impossible. She checked her e-mail every five minutes.

Finally, right before she was about to go to bed, she
got something.

To: mad4u

From: p_diddy

Re: date?

A chick from that dating game site matched me with you. r u
up for it? want to meet at the pinetop Saturday night? I
mean, why wait, right?

The Pinetop! Wow. Saturday night—she'd have to miss Rebecca's party. Oh well. This was way better than some lame party. Going to the Pinetop Lounge with Sean Benedetto!

The Pinetop was a divey old bar known for its ancient jukebox and lax door policy. Mads had heard some of the older kids at Rosewood talk about it. Holly's sister Piper used to go there all the time. They hardly ever carded. Still, Mads knew she looked closer to twelve than twenty-one, and that might test the Pinetop's limits. She needed a fake ID—now. It was time to get one, anyway.

Mads wrote back to Sean:

Pinetop's cool. See you at 8?
Saturday night at 8. See you then. How will I know you?

I'll know you, she wanted to say, but thought better of it. Instead she wrote:

I have straight black hair. You've probably seen me around
    school.

Next she fired off an e-mail to Holly.

Emergency—I need a fake id now! Can Piper hook me up?
    I'm about to go on my very first date with SEAN
    BENEDETTO!!!!

10 Nightmare at the Pinetop Lounge

To:	mad4u
From:	Your daily horoscope

HERE IS TODAY'S HOROSCOPE: VIRGO: You have strong ideals, Virgo, and that's a good thing. But watch out—reality is about to bite you in the butt.

Mads' seat belt could hardly restrain her as M.C. piloted the Volvo through the hills to Ridgewood Road. The Pinetop Lodge stood at the end of a small, isolated commercial strip, with a gas station, an old convenience store, a deli, and Prescott's Pizza Shop.

"There it is, Mom," Mads said. "Prescott's."

M.C. pulled into the parking lot. A few doors down, the Pinetop was hopping.

"Are you sure this is where you're meeting this boy?" M.C. asked.

"Sure, Mom," Mads said. She'd told M.C. that Sean was meeting her for pizza. M.C. was very liberal in a lot of ways: She believed in human rights and freedom for people all over the globe and all kinds of animals. But when it came to her daughter, certain rights didn't apply. That included the right to go to a bar with a boy at age fifteen. Mads tried to argue that her parents' rules made her a political prisoner, but they weren't that stupid.

"Is he here yet?" M.C. asked, looking around. Two cars were parked in front of Prescott's, and a few people stood at the counter inside. "I think I'll wait with you until he gets here. Just to make sure you're all right."

"Mom, no!" Mads cried. "I don't want him to think I need my mother to drive me around."

"But you're not old enough to drive yourself! How is he going to think you got here in the first place?"

"Please, Mom. Look, I've got my cell phone." Mads opened her bag and flashed her new cell phone as if to demonstrate. "If he doesn't show up or anything goes wrong, I'll call you. I promise."

"All right," M.C. said. "But call me as soon as he shows up. If I don't hear from you in fifteen minutes, I'm calling you. And if you don't answer, I'm coming right back."

"Thanks, Mom." Mads opened the door and got out of the car at last.

"Home by midnight!" M.C. reminded her.

Mads went into Prescott's and watched her mom drive off. Then she went into the bathroom, put on some lipstick, and headed over to the Pinetop.

No sign of the Jeep yet. Mads figured she'd wait for Sean outside. It started to drizzle, so she waited under the Pinetop awning.

After a few minutes a black Jeep pulled up, and Sean got out. In the light of the streetlamp Mads watched him shake out his hair, stuff his keys in his pocket and head for the door. Mads positioned herself in front of it so he couldn't miss her.

"Hi," he said, reaching around her for the handle to the door. She blocked him.

"Hi," she said. "Are you meeting someone here?"

His eyes narrowed as he stopped to take her in. "Yeah, I am, but—"

"Is your screen name 'p_diddy'?" Mads asked.

His jaw fell open. "Are you 'mad4u'?"

"That's me. My real name is Madison."

He stared at her, jaw hanging down, for a full three seconds. "You're my date?"

"Yep."

"But you're just a kid!"

Mads started to panic. He wasn't joking. He really seemed shocked and unhappy to see her.

"No, I'm not!" she insisted. "I'm a sophomore! I'm fifteen!"

"You are?" He took a step back and pushed his bangs up with his hand. "You don't look that old."

"But I am, I swear," she said. She reached for her wallet, which held her brand new fake ID. Holly's sister Piper had gotten one for each of them. "You want to see my ID? Well, actually, it says I'm twenty-one, which I'm not, but it has my picture on it!"

Sean laughed a little. "Look, kid," he said. "You're cute and all, but you're a little young for me."

"Why don't you just give me a chance?" Mads pleaded. "I mean, we're here now. Can't we go inside and talk? Maybe once you get to know me you'll see—"

"Okay, okay, calm down." Sean seemed eager to get out of the rain. "Come on, let's go in."

He opened the door and ushered her inside. It was dark, but as her eyes adjusted Mads saw an old, scarred wooden bar, wood floors dotted with cigarette burns, neon beer signs everywhere, a jukebox, and a pool table in the back. High school kids—some she recognized and some she didn't—were clustered at the bar and a few rickety tables. Two overweight men in their fifties claimed one end of the bar as their territory. The kids steered clear of them.

"It's the S-man!" a guy at the bar called out to Sean. The guy was talking to two girls on bar stools. Mads didn't recognize them. They looked a little older, as if they could have been in college.

"Hey, Rich, I thought you might be here." Sean slapped his hand against Rich's and they did a kind of pseudo-hip-hop handshake. He took a step to the side and jostled Mads. "Oh, this is, uh—what was your name again?"

"Madison," Mads said. "Madison Markowitz."

"Madison." Sean nodded. "Let's get you a drink. What'll you have?"

Mads hesitated. She'd had wine at Holly's house and beer at parties, but that was about it. She looked around and saw that most people in the bar were drinking beer.

"I'll have a Rolling Rock," she said.

"Great." Sean gestured to the bartender, a bony young man with a thin pencil mustache. "A Rolling Rock and an Anchor Steam."

The bartender looked at Mads. "Uh, how old is she?"

Sean didn't answer, just glanced back at her. "I'm twenty-one," she said in a squeaky, unconvincing voice.

"Oh, really? Let me see your ID."

"Wow, nobody ever gets carded in this place," Rich murmured to the girls. Mads dug through her wallet and handed over her ID. Take that! The bartender held it under the light over the cash register. Then he chuckled and handed it back to her. "There's no way you're twenty-one. Nice try, though. Sorry, man. She can't stay."

Can't stay? No! What good was a fake ID if no one believed it?

"What if I just get a Coke or something?" Mads asked. "I won't drink any alcohol."

"No minors allowed. I can't even serve you water."

"Are you kidding?" Sean brushed his hair back in frustration. "Man, this sucks."

"Get her out of here and don't give me any trouble," the bartender said.

"Come on, kid." Sean stalked back to the door. Madison followed him.

"What are we going to do?" she asked.

"What choice do we have? You're going to go home, that's what."

"But what about our date?"

"How can I date a girl who can't even get into the Pinetop? I've been going there since I was thirteen!" He shuffled and stamped his feet. "I can't date you if I can't take you out, can I?"

We could go somewhere else, even Prescott's, Mads thought sadly, but didn't say it. He wanted what he wanted, and she was getting in the way. She shrank up inside, remembering how she'd felt when Yucky Gilbert showed up for their date. Was that how Sean felt about her?

"Does your mom know you're here?" Sean asked.

"My mom!" Mads was indignant. "She doesn't care what I do. She's a drug dealer." She didn't know what made her lie. It just popped out.

Sean laughed. "Your mother's a drug dealer? I don't believe you."

"Okay, she's not a drug dealer. I just lied because I didn't want to tell you the truth: My mom ran away to become a stripper. And my dad's a pimp. I'm basically an orphan."

"Cut it out," Sean said. "You're funny, but you're still too young for me."

"I don't get it," Mads said. "You dated Lulu Ramos last fall. We're the same age. She's in my class!"

"Really?" Sean looked surprised, as if she and Lulu Ramos couldn't even be from the same planet. Lulu, it was true, wore lots of makeup, was always being sent home for dress code violations (bare midriffs, plunging necklines, microminis, and vinyl catsuits weren't allowed at Rosewood), and was very sure of herself around boys. "That was different. Lulu seems a lot older than you. She's, you know, more experienced. Maybe it's because her mother was an Aerosmith groupie, I don't know . . ."

Mads' heart sank. The cause was lost, for that night at least. She knew when she was beaten.

"Look, it's nothing personal," Sean said. "Trust me, I'm

doing you a favor. So, where's your car? I'll walk you."

Ugh. The ultimate humiliation. "I don't have a car. I can't drive yet."

"Oh. Well, how are you going to get home?"

"I—I guess I'll call someone to come pick me up." Mads' phone beeped at that moment. It was M.C., calling to check on her. Mads took a few steps away from Sean for privacy. Maybe he had to know her mother was picking her up, but he didn't have to hear her ask for it.

"Sorry, Mom—can you come back and get me?" Mads said, choking back tears.

"Of course, honey. Is everything all right?"

"It's fine. But Sean called at the last minute and said he couldn't make it. We're going to reschedule."

"I'll be right there."

"Um, I have to wait for her at Prescott's," Mads told Sean. "She doesn't like me to go to bars."

"I'll go over there and wait with you," Sean said.

They perched on a picnic table under a yellow plastic awning and watched the cars swish by in the drizzle. Mads hoped at least they'd get to talk for a few minutes while they waited, but Sean's cell phone rang. He answered it and started talking to his friend Alex. Mads sat and listened. "Dude, the Pinetop's pretty quiet tonight," Sean said over the phone. "But you should come by. That cute girl from Mill Valley is there. . . ."

Her mother pulled up in the Volvo, windshield wipers flapping. "That her?" Sean said. "The drug-dealing stripper?"

"Yeah. Thanks, Sean. See you around."

"See you." He nodded at M.C. through the window. Mads got up and ran to the passenger door and climbed inside. M.C. had the radio on, new wave oldies.

"Who's that boy?" M.C. asked. "I thought Sean didn't show up."

"That's just a friend of mine from school," Mads said. "Can we go home now?"

M.C. peered into Mads' face. "Is everything okay, honey? Are you disappointed about your date?"

Mads tried to turn her features to stone. She didn't feel like breaking down over this in front of her mother. It would only add to the embarrassment.

"Honey?"

"No, Mom," she snapped. "Don't get all touchy-feely with me. Can we just go, please?"

"Sorry. Sorry. Sorry." M.C. backed up the Volvo, pulled out into the street, and drove Madison home. Mads glanced back. Sean had already disappeared into the bar.

linaonme: he should have taken you somewhere else.
Someplace it's not illegal for you to set foot in.
hollygolitely: he's an asshole.
mad4u: no he's not! I love him. even if he's an asshole. But

he's wrong about me. I'm not too young for him!

linaonme: all right! Fight for your man!

mad4u: u know what the problem is? I'm not experienced
enough. That's what it is! He can see it on my face! he
can tell I'm a virgin!

hollygolitely: I think you're giving him too much credit.

mad4u: no. the questionnaires proved it. everybody else in
school has way more experience than me. now it's my
turn. I'm going to show Sean I'm not some little kid. I'm
a mature, sensual woman. Or I will be, as soon as I get
a little experience. It will show on my face. Right?

linaonme: brilliant idea mads. sure to work.

hollygolitely: it's totally crackpot.

mad4u: doubters. You'll see. I'll become a woman, and sean
won't be able to resist me. the only question is, how do I
do it?

Mads logged onto the Dating Game chat room,
using the screen name snow_white.

snow_white: students of rsage! I need your help. I'm a 15-
year-old girl and I'm a virgin! I need some experience—
now! what's the best way to hook up with a boy?

r2d2: why don't you just walk around naked?

digger90: who are you? I'll take care of your little problem.

simsfan2: I know a secret potion that will make any boy fall in

love with you. mix pomegranate juice with 3 cloves, a
pinch of nutmeg, and 3 hairs from a burmese cat. Heat
it on the stove. Spit in it. Add jello mix. Raspberry only.
Refrigerate for 3 days. On the third day, chant this spell
over the bowl—heema hama heema hama. Serve to
your victim. He will become your love slave.

digger90: What are you, ugly?

tanaquil: go up to the boy you like and lick his hand. it's an
animal signal. His primal urges will come out but he
won't know what's happening to him.

roto: call him on the phone late at night, breathing heavily.
Don't tell him who you are at first. His imagination will
start to go crazy. He'll have to have you.

breaker19: wear those super-low-cut jeans and a tiny top.
Shouldn't take too long.

redmenace: find a really desperate boy, close your eyes, hold
your nose, and think of viggo mortensen.

digger90: just pick a guy and lunge.

Digger90 made more sense than anyone, Mads thought. *Just
pick a guy and go for it.* Why not? The perfect opportunity
was less than a week away. Mariska Frasier's party on
Saturday night. It was no big deal—Mariska was a sophomore, so Sean would only show up if there was nothing
better to do that night. But it was a good chance to put
some of this advice to the test.

Hot for Teacher

To:	linaonme
From:	Your daily horoscope

HERE IS TODAY'S HOROSCOPE: CANCER: The bad news: Today you will sink to a new low. The good news: You won't hit rock bottom—for a few weeks.

All right, Karl, let's hear your latest proposal."
Dan leaned against the front of his desk with his patient face on, but Lina could tell he was struggling. Karl Levine still hadn't decided what to do for his IHD project. Dan had rejected all his ideas so far, with good reason: they were all dumb, and most were illegal. Spying on his sister in the bathroom, putting a camera in the girls' locker room, trying to get a date with his mother's manicurist. Lina felt sorry for Dan that he had to pretend

to tolerate so much stupidity. At the same time, she admired him for keeping his cool.

Karl stood up and cleared his throat. "Okay, here's my proposal: I buy a blow-up sex doll. Her name is Friendly Fanny. I put her in the front seat of my car and drive down the highway during rush hour *in the HOV lane*. You know, that lane where you have to have at least two people in the car or you get a ticket? And see if I get away with it."

He sat down with a smug grin on his face. He was unshame-able.

A pained look crossed Dan's face. He sighed and stood up. He turned away from the class and rubbed his temples. When he turned around again, his face was composed.

"Sorry, Karl. Rejected. Look, forget about spying on people and blow-up dolls and think of a real research project. If you need help, come speak to me after class. But do it soon. You'd better settle on a project by next Friday or you're in danger of failing this class."

Lina was glad to see Dan come down hard on Karl—it was about time. The first semester he'd been all smiley and buddy-buddy, but this semester seemed to be taking a toll on him. He had a new crease across his forehead. Lina worried about him. He was stressed.

Dan glanced at a paper on his desk. "Okay, let's hear from 'Grupo Ocho.' Ramona, Chandra, Siobhan, and Maggie."

Lina braced herself. Ramona's group was doing a project on fashion and the use of clothes to send sexual signals, but they had gotten a little off-track. Basically they looked at what people in various cliques wore and dissed them.

Ramona read from her paper. "This week Grupo Ocho found that the most popular girls in the school are all mindless followers. For example, if a girl who is not in their group tries a fashion innovation—that is, wears something new and experimental, like an earring made out of her little sister's bloody baby tooth—the popular girls ignore it. But if their lead girl wears something just as unusual—"

Or gross, Lina thought.

"—like a bracelet made of safety pins, all her friends copy her right away. In conclusion, it doesn't matter what you're wearing. What matters is *who's wearing it*."

Ooh. Deep, Holly scribbled in the margin of Lina's notebook.

"Uh, all right, good," Dan said. "I have a suggestion, Grupo Ocho. Your project would be greatly enhanced by drawings or photos. So everyone could see the fashion examples you write about in your report. What do you think?"

"That's a brilliant idea, Dan," Ramona said. "We'll definitely do that." She beamed at him. Her friends did too, but Ramona was clearly the most far-gone. It made Lina sick.

Mads made a jokey face at Lina, pursing her lips and moving them ever so slightly, mimicking suck-up Ramona. Lina thought it was funny but couldn't bring herself to laugh. Watching Ramona was like seeing herself in a funhouse mirror—her own feelings for Dan, distorted. But there was still truth in that distorted reflection. Lina and Ramona had different styles but the same core—they both loved Dan. It drove Lina crazy.

Lina unlocked her bike at the end of the school day and pedaled across the parking lot. A car pulled in front of her and she stopped and glanced back. Dan knelt by the bike rack, unlocking his own bike. He was leaving school earlier than usual. Lina wondered where he was going. Home? Off to do errands?

He strapped on his helmet and biked away in the opposite direction, down the front walk leading away from the school entrance. Lina didn't think. She just followed him.

It was easy. He never looked back. She stayed half a block behind him as he rode down Rosewood Avenue toward the water. Down the hill, right on Rutgers Street to a waterfront café called the Bayside. A gray, weather-beaten boardwalk lined with benches ran along the water, separating the café from the piers.

Dan locked his bike at a rack in front of the café. He

scanned the outdoor deck and waved at a good-looking dark-haired woman sitting alone at a table under a heat lamp. He leaped up three steps to the deck and joined her.

Lina walked her bike to a bench across from the café. She leaned the bike against the bench and sat down. She told herself she was tired from the fifteen-minute bike ride from school to the waterfront, but she knew that was a lie. Now that she'd started this spying thing, she had to see it through to the end. Who was the woman? His girlfriend? A date? His sister? Just a friend?

She rummaged through her backpack, found her sunglasses, and put them on, hoping they'd be enough of a disguise to keep him from noticing her. Not that there seemed to be any danger of that. Since he'd sat down, he'd barely taken his eyes off the dark-haired girl.

Lina studied her carefully. She definitely wasn't his sister. She was about his age, twenty-three or twenty-four, and her almost-black hair brushed her collarbone, shiny and thick with a slight wave. A cream-colored sweater was tied over her shoulders and large, dark, expensive-looking sunglasses perched on top of her head. She sat back in her wicker chair, comfortable and confident, chatting easily. Dan leaned forward, listening to her closely and nodding.

Lina wished she could get closer to hear what they were saying. Should she try to get a table at the café? No, Dan would definitely notice her then and feel uncomfortable.

The woman stood up. She picked up a large leather bag and walked inside the café. Probably going to the ladies' room. Lina got a glimpse of her whole outfit then—a cream-colored knit tank top that matched her sweater, which she pulled on over the tank top now, a chunky gold necklace, a pair of neat white pants, and high heeled sandals. Everything looked expensive to Lina's eye, and she knew expensive clothes. Her mother had a closet full of them.

While the woman was gone, Dan gazed out toward the water. Lina stood up and walked her bike away, afraid he'd spot her. She went to a coffee stand and got a coffee to go. When she returned to her spying spot on the bench, the woman was back from the bathroom. A waiter set drinks in front of them.

Lina sipped her hot coffee while she watched. Now the date didn't seem to be going so well. The woman wasn't talking as much as she did at first. The uncomfortable silences between her and Dan grew longer. Could this be a first date—or a blind date? Lina thought back to her own last date, with Walker. The awkwardness she saw between Dan and this woman looked awfully familiar.

Something fluttered to Lina's left, a flap of black fabric. She turned to see a pasty-faced Ramona lurking nearby, huddled under a black cape. Lina nearly dropped her coffee. She was caught! No, she'd deny it. There was no law against sitting on a bench by the bay drinking coffee on a Friday afternoon.

"Spying again?" Ramona sneered.

"What are you doing here?" Lina asked.

"I've been lurking by the newsstand for a while now," she said. "If I sat right out in the open like you, Dan would notice me for sure. Of course, I stand out more than you do."

Yeah, but not in a good way, Lina thought.

"What about you?" Lina asked. "Are *you* spying?"

"I don't think of it as spying," Ramona said. "When one loves as I do, fully, deeply, completely—one cannot be blamed for anything one does, for it is all in the service of the highest of human aspirations—true spiritual communion."

Lina rolled her eyes. Ramona sat down beside her. "Aren't you afraid he'll see you?" Lina asked.

"Not anymore. He's totally into this chick. Luckily for me, she doesn't like him that much. I mean, luckily for us." She cast a meaningful look at Lina, who cringed. There was no denying she'd had the same thought.

"Look—she's leaving," Lina said as the woman stood up and grabbed her bag. Dan stood up politely. She shook his hand. Not even a peck on the cheek.

"She's leaving him to pay the check," Ramona noted. The woman strode down the steps and down the walk toward the waterway path where the girls sat watching her. She cast a dismissive glance at Dan's bike, the only one locked to the rack by the steps.

"Superficial bitch," Ramona muttered. Lina had to agree.

The woman walked around to a parking lot next to the café. She pressed her key ring—her car alarm deactivated with a *squawk*—got into a Mercedes convertible and drove off.

Dan sat alone on the deck. He rattled the ice in his drink, sucked on the straw. He looked lonely.

Lina's heart went out to him. How could that woman hurt him like this? She wanted to run to him and say, "You don't need her! She's not good enough for you!"

The waiter brought Dan the check. He put some bills on the table and got up to leave.

"We'd better move or he'll see us," Ramona said. "Come on, the newsstand."

Lina wheeled her bike and hid with Ramona behind the newsstand. They peeked around to watch Dan put on his helmet, unlock his bike and ride away.

Lina wished she could follow him home, to see where he lived, but she wouldn't do it with Ramona right there.

But maybe some other time . . .

12 The Male Mind Is Impervious to Logic

To:	hollygolitely, linaonme, mad4u
From:	Your daily horoscope

HERE IS TODAY'S HOROSCOPE: LUNAR ECLIPSE! This is such a huge astrological event that it will affect all the signs in the zodiac. Alliances will shift, secrets will be revealed, identities will change. Go out tonight—if you stay home you'll miss the fun!

I like your new punk look, Mads," Holly said in the car on the way to Mariska's. "It's so not you."

Mads had put lots of goop in her hair to make it messy, smudged her makeup, and tore holes in her t-shirt and tights.

"Tonight's the night," Mads said. "I'm roughing up my image. After tonight, there'll be a new Madison Markowitz in town. When you think of me, you'll think *bad girl*."

"We could call you 'Bad Mads,'" Holly said. "Or 'Maddie the Baddie.' Would that help?"

"No," Mads said.

Mads, Lina, and Holly walked into Mariska's party at 10:30, when it was already going strong. Claire and Ingrid lounged by the living room door, smoking. "Ooh, can I bum one?" Mads asked. Bad girls smoked, so she should, too.

Claire dug one out of her pack, complaining, "Do you know how expensive these are?"

"I'll send you a check," Mads said. "Thanks, Claire."

Ingrid lit it for her. Mads took a puff. Ugh. The nicotine hit her blood stream and landed with a sickening thud in her stomach.

"You're turning green," Ingrid said.

"Give me that." Claire snatched the cigarette away from Mads. "You don't smoke. You're just wasting it!"

Mads gladly relinquished the butt. So she wasn't a smoker. Fine. Smoking wasn't the only thing a bad girl could do.

"Have you seen Jake yet?" Lina asked Holly.

"No," Holly said. "But I see Karl Levine brought a date."

Karl Levine sat on the living room couch with the Friendly Fanny blow-up sex doll he'd talked about in IHD class. "I guess she's about the best Karl can do, date-wise,"

Lina said. "They should be here," she added, meaning Jake and Walker. "Walker told me he was coming."

Holly was nervous about seeing Jake. It had been two weeks since their double date with Lina and Walker. Jake never called. When she saw him at school, he said hi but not much else. She had a bad feeling. But maybe she was misreading him. Who could tell what a guy was thinking? Their minds seemed completely impervious to logic.

Walker, on the other hand, made it clear that he liked Lina, even though he didn't push her. He'd already called her twice. And Lina didn't care! It bugged Holly a little. She tried to play it cool like Lina. Why wasn't it working for her?

"What's with your friend Madison?" Sebastiano, wearing tight striped jeans and a leather jacket, materialized in front of them. He nodded at Mads, who was dancing wildly in front of three boys who gaped at her as if she were on crazy pills. "Is she channeling Courtney Love?"

"She's trying to change her image," Holly explained.

"Hmm. I think I can help her," Sebastiano said. "I know the perfect guy—he's an instant reputation-wrecker, and he's conveniently here tonight. Dashiell Piasecki."

"Who's that?" Lina asked.

Sebastiano pointed to a tallish guy across the room with blocky shoulders and the boyishly conservative haircut of a politician. His blue polo shirt was tucked into his belted jeans.

"That guy?" Lina said. "I always thought he looked so uptight."

"He's a junior," Sebastiano explained. "He might look like a golf pro, but word is he's a player. He goes after anything that moves, as long as it's female. Even better, he can't keep his mouth shut. If Mads wants her little adventure advertised, Dash is your guy."

"Looks like Mads has already sniffed him out," Holly said. Across the room, Dash was pouring on the charm and Mads was giggling.

Lina elbowed Holly. "Hey—there's Sean." Sean walked through the living room, right past Mads and Dash.

Mads sensed Sean's presence from the moment he stepped into the room. She watched him out of the corner of her eye, all the while talking and flirting with Dash. *Look at me, Sean,* she telegraphed. *This boy is a junior and he's flirting with me. He doesn't think I'm too young.* Sean glanced at Mads as he passed, then did a double-take. All right! He noticed her! He even recognized her through all the wild hair and makeup. But all he said was, "Hey, kid. What's up?" Mads wanted to melt, even though she had the feeling he couldn't remember her name.

That was okay. By the end of the night she'd make a name for herself, and he'd remember it.

"Hey," Dash said. "Want a beer? Let me get you a beer."

Mads followed him out to the keg on the back porch, where he poured two generous cups of beer. "Drink up," Dash said, guzzling his.

"Yeah. Party!" Mads took a sip.

"You're a cool girl," Dash said. "I can tell."

"Thanks." He poured himself another beer and squirted a bit more into her cup, even though she'd hardly made a dent in it.

"I wish they served decent wine at these parties," Holly complained. She and Lina were raiding the kitchen, looking for something to drink besides beer.

Through the open screen door they could hear the voices of people gathered around the keg on the back porch. "I had to get cable so I could watch Manchester United on ITN," a low voice said.

Holly grabbed Lina. "It's Jake!" she whispered. Talking about soccer as usual.

"What's Manchester United?" a girl's voice said. "Is it like an airline or something?"

"What do I do?" Holly whispered. "Should I say something? Should I ignore him? What should I do?"

"Shh! Someone's coming!" Lina whispered as the screen door squeaked open. Jake, two other guys, and a girl walked into the kitchen, clutching beers. Jake cast a quick glance at Holly but said nothing. One of the girls opened the fridge and grabbed a few Diet Cokes. Then the group headed back outside and across the yard to the pool house.

"I can't believe he did that!" Lina cried. "He just walked right by without saying hello or anything!"

"I know." Holly's heart beat heavily against her breastbone. She was about to do something stupid, and she knew it. The worst part was she couldn't stop herself. The little Nancy Drew inside her always had to solve the mystery. Jake was acting weird and she had to know why.

"Hi, girls." Walker appeared, beer in hand. "How's it going?"

Holly tried to smile at him, but it was hard. His friendliness only underlined Jake's coldness toward her.

"Hi, Walker," Lina said. "Listen, do you know what's up with Jake? He's giving us the freeze. Ow!"

Holly mashed Lina's toe with the tip of her shoe. She didn't want Lina to tell Walker what was going on. She didn't want anyone to know. But it was too late. Anyway, Lina got the message—she wouldn't talk about it with anyone else.

"Really? That's weird," Walker said. "I don't know. I'm not really close to him or anything. . . ."

"I'm going out to the pool house," Holly said.

"I'll come with you," Lina said.

"No—you stay here with Walker," Holly said.

"Holly—"

"I mean it."

Lina watched Holly walk out the back door. She was worried about her. What was wrong with Jake? How could he treat Holly this way?

The pool house was a different scene from the main house—louder, darker, smokier. A few kids lingered by the pool, but it was a chilly night and most people took shelter inside. Jake looked up when Holly appeared, then looked away. He whispered something to his friends. One of the girls giggled. Holly wanted to turn around and run, but she stood her ground.

They were talking about her. But why? She'd hardly fooled around with Jake—there was nothing to say about their flop of a date the week before. But why should that stop anyone?

Holly stood at the edge of the room, alone, wondering what to do. A few kids bopped to a hip-hop CD. A trio of guys leaned against the wood paneling, talking, laughing, and looking her way. What were they expecting from her, a striptease? She walked boldly into the room as if their stupid rumors didn't scare her.

Sebastiano snaked toward her, smoking a cigarette. "Hey, beautiful," he said, leading Holly to a couch. "So, the details of your blind date are out. As your locker-neighbor, from now on, I'd really appreciate if I could hear these things directly from you, so *I* can be the one spreading it around."

Holly steadied her nerves. "What details are you talking about?"

"Your super-hot date with Jake, of course. Apparently that rack of yours is amazing. According to Jake, you have earned the title of Boobmeister General, every inch of it." He half-bowed toward her. She wanted to kick him.

"Let's see," Sebastiano continued. "You danced naked in front of him at his house, then you pounced on him and made wild, passionate love for hours. He finally had to drag you home by the hair, but you kept begging for more. . . ."

"He dragged me by the hair?"

"Okay, that little touch is mine," Sebastiano admitted. "But the rest of it is pure hearsay."

Holly couldn't believe Jake was saying this. There wasn't even one kernel of truth in it! She was never at his house, they were at Walker's, and all they did was kiss a little. And he was a terrible kisser!

She didn't get it. What did he want—to make it look as if he'd used her and dropped her? Was that supposed to make him look good somehow? Was he embarrassed because nothing happened on their date? That was his own fault!

She would never understand guys.

Two girls walked by, talking closely. "Which one is she?" one girl asked the other as they brushed past Holly's knees.

"Shh! She's right there!" the other whispered, loud enough for Holly to hear. They scurried away, giggling.

"So Jake's trying to ride your rep to a bad-boy rep of his own," Sebastiano said. "Age-old ploy. Of course, it will probably backfire once I start spreading your side of the story. But I have to warn you that people may not buy it. Not that it's not believable. It's just not as much fun to talk about."

"Whatever." Holly started to feel uncomfortable, the smoky, noisy, crowded pool house closing in on her. "I need some air."

She pulled herself off the couch and went outside. She sat on a bench by the pool and wished she'd brought her jacket with her.

She knew about the double standard, how it was good for boys to have a wild rep and bad for girls. But why didn't Jake just date her, instead of making up stories? Was he afraid of her? And then she saw an answer. If she dated Jake steadily—if she was Jake's girlfriend—then she wouldn't be a slut anymore. And Jake wouldn't be a stud, he'd just be a guy with a girlfriend. He probably wasn't ready for a girlfriend, anyway.

Rob Safran, one of the boys she'd noticed in the pool house, walked over and sat down on the bench. "Hey," he said. "Are you okay?"

She glanced up at him, surprised. She knew who he

was—they were both on the Community Service Committee, along with about a hundred other kids. She'd never given him much thought, but now that she looked at him she thought he was kind of cute. His thick, messy brown hair stuck out around his head as if he cut it himself. He had brown eyes and broad cheekbones that might have looked severe if it weren't for the freckles dotting them all over, which made him look boyish and sweet.

But what was he doing here? Her antennae shot up warily—had he come to tease her? Torture her? Play some kind of joke? Time to bring back the tough girl act.

He sat down next to her. "You left the pool house kind of suddenly."

"Everything's cool," she said. "I just needed some air. And that Nelly song was getting to me. If I hear it one more time I'm going to lose it."

"Yeah, some stoner kept hitting repeat on the stereo," Rob said. "You're one of the girls who started that blog, aren't you? The Dating Game? With those questionnaires and the matchmaking and everything, right?"

"Right," Holly said. "It's an IHD project."

"God, IHD. What a stupid class. I took it last year. They should be honest and call it HWT: Huge Waste of Time."

"What was your project?" Holly asked.

"I—don't want to tell you. It's too embarrassing."

"Come on! What was it? I won't laugh, I promise."

"Well—remember, last year was Dan's first year teaching, so he didn't know what he was doing. He approved just about everything—"

"Tell me!"

"Okay. I studied my dad's dating habits. Who he dated, how long it lasted, what they did on their dates, what my mom had to say about it . . ."

"I guess they're divorced."

"It would be pretty sad if they weren't."

"What grade did you get on it?" Holly asked.

"A. Doesn't everybody get an A in IHD?"

Holly shrugged. "I don't know. Maybe Dan's getting tougher this year."

She felt better now. Maybe it was the fresh air. But it was also the way Rob was talking to her. He must have heard the rumors Jake was spreading, but he acted as if he didn't believe a word of it. Still, she reminded herself, it could be just that—an act.

"It must be pretty late," she said, getting to her feet. "I'd better go in and find my friends."

"I'll go with you." Rob followed her inside. A few heads turned and noted that Rob and Holly had just been outside together. Holly could read it on their faces. But no one said a thing.

She found Lina and Walker, who told her Mads had disappeared with Dashiell. "She's in the den," Lina said.

"You know that room Mariska said nobody was allowed to go into?"

"Ya know, you're so cute I could bite your little nose off," Dash said, slurring his words. His head bobbed and he squinted at her through half-shut eyes. Mads figured he must have had six beers, easy.

"Thanks," she said. She'd thought he was cute, too, at one point. Yes, she remembered thinking he was cute earlier in the evening. But now she thought he was a big idiot with beer breath.

She sat in Mariska's father's forbidden den, the most private place they could find (since Mariska had roped off the upstairs), pressed into an easy chair, with Dash on top of her.

"Ya know what? I really want to kiss you, you cute little thing." Dash licked her nose, then kissed her wetly on the lips. She squirmed under him, trying to keep his elbow from squashing her stomach. He clutched at her back, feeling for a bra strap. Then he reached under her shirt and unsnapped her bra. Mads had the feeling he'd done this before, lots of times.

"Um, could you get off me?" she said. "My legs are falling asleep."

He grinned down at her. "You're so great," he said, kissing her again. "Yeah. Ya know? Yeah."

"What?" she asked. He was muttering, not making much sense. He kissed her throat and started nuzzling her neck. Then, suddenly, he stopped. His weight pressed down heavily on her.

"Dash?" Mads said. "What are you doing?"

He didn't answer. He didn't move. She grabbed a hunk of his hair and lifted his head and stared at him. "Dash?"

He let out a snore. Oh, great. He was passed out on top of her!

He's supposed to be the horniest guy in school, Mads thought as she wriggled out from under him, *and he falls asleep on me!* But maybe it was just as well. At that moment, she found him kind of disgusting.

She redid her bra and straightened her clothes. She left him snoring and drooling facedown on the easy chair.

"Mads! What's going on?" Lina asked when Mads reappeared in the living room. Lina left Walker in the corner and dragged Mads into the hallway for privacy.

"Absolutely nothing," Mads said. "And I mean absolutely *nothing.*"

"You mean you didn't . . . you know . . ."

"He passed out. He's wasted."

"Bummer," Lina said, but she was secretly relieved. She knew Mads was doing all this for Sean, but somehow the idea of Mads and Dash just didn't sit right. Mads and Dash. Mad Dash. Huh. That was funny.

"Sean left the party a long time ago, anyway," Lina told her.

"He left?" Mads said, disappointed. "Do you think he wondered where I was? Did he say anything?"

"Not to me," Lina said. "He doesn't really talk to me."

"Me either," Mads said.

"Here comes Holly," Lina said.

"Oh! What happened with Jake?" Mads whispered.

"Fill you in later," Lina whispered back. "I think there's a new development."

"You guys ready to go soon?" Holly asked.

"I could give you a ride home," Rob said to Holly.

"Thanks, but I drove," Holly said. "And I've got to give these two a ride." She introduced Rob to Mads and Lina.

"That's cool," Rob said. "Well, see you at school." He smiled at her so warmly that Jake melted out of her system for good. Even the buzz Jake had generated died down. Now everyone was wondering if Rob and Holly were hooking up.

Holly, Lina, and Mads headed for the car. "So?" Holly asked Mads. "Are you a fallen woman?"

"No," Mads said. "I'm so unsexy even the horniest guy in school can't stay awake in my presence. What's going on, Holly? What's with this guy Rob?"

"In the car," Holly said. "I'll tell you all about it."

13 Outie in Disguise

HERE IS TODAY'S HOROSCOPE: VIRGO: Somebody out there likes you, Virgo. It's nice to be liked, right?

I don't get it," Audrey said. She was lounging, uninvited, on Mads' bed Sunday morning. Mads sat at her computer, reading over the new Dating Game entries. Some people wanted to be anonymous, but others were attaching photos to their questionnaires, like personal ads.

"If you're in love with Sean Benedetto, why do you want a different boyfriend?" Audrey asked.

Mads was not about to explain the whole virginity thing to her eleven-year-old sister. That was M.C.'s assignment, should she choose to accept it.

"How is this any of your business?" Mads asked. "What are you doing in my room, anyway? And get your stinkola slippers off my bed!"

Audrey pouted and slid her dirty, pink fuzzy-bunny slippers over the edge of the bed, just enough to obey the letter of the law. "Come on, Mads, I'm bored," she whined. "Don't you want to do something? I hate Sundays."

"I'm busy. Go bug the Overlord to play a video game with you."

"He said he would after he's finished reading the paper," Audrey said. "The paper that never ends. He'll still be reading it at breakfast tomorrow." She slid off the bed and stood behind Mads, looking over her shoulder at the computer screen. "Why are you looking at a picture of some girl's belly button?"

A girl screen-named "queenie" had submitted a picture of her midriff—and only her midriff—along with her questionnaire. It wasn't a bad idea, Mads thought. It was a pretty cute midriff.

"What is this?" Audrey asked. "Is this that project you're doing with Holly and Lina?"

"Yes. Now shut up. Or go away. Or both."

"Why don't you do an ad?" Audrey suggested. "Maybe Sean will see it and he'll ask you out. Don't put your belly button in the picture, though. It looks like Grandpa's face."

"It does not," Mads said. She pulled up her shirt and examined her belly button. It did look a little like an old man's shriveled face. But she'd never admit it. "At least I don't have an outie like you."

"It popped in a long time ago!" Audrey huffed.

"It's still an outie in disguise," Mads said. Audrey was very sensitive about this. It was an easy way for Mads to get to her. "Outie freak."

But Audrey's idea wasn't bad. Why not post an ad on the blog? An ad that made her seem worldly, experienced, and sexy. Maybe people would start treating her differently. Maybe Sean would see it and it would change his mind. Maybe he'd even ask her out! The key was a sexy photo.

She looked at Audrey, a faithful Britney Spears disciple from the age of six. Even on Sunday, just hanging at home, Audrey wore an armload of bright plastic bangles, a flower choker, eye shadow and lip gloss with her pink flannel pajamas—sleeves and legs rolled trendily up, of course. The girl was only eleven, but Mads knew Audrey had a lot to teach her big sister about being a pop tart.

"Get Mom's digital camera, Aud," Mads said. "You're going to take my picture for my personal ad."

Mads made herself up as glamorously as she could and posed in a tube top, her lips puckered in a kiss. Audrey snapped a few shots. Mads picked the best one and loaded it onto the computer, wrote her ad, and submitted it.

Screen Name: mad4u

Age: 15

Grade: 10

Looking for: love! With a boy. I like older boys, especially
seniors. I'm very sophisticated and experienced.
Remember, good things come in small packages. Not
that I'm small or anything.

Now all she had to do was wait for the love to start
pouring in.

"Mads' personal ad gave me an idea for a new quiz," Holly
said to Lina as they headed for the library. "Something like,
'Do You Know How to Decode a Personal Ad?'"

"Like, when Mads says she's very experienced, she
really means she wishes she were?" Lina said.

"Exactly."

Lina sat at a computer terminal in the library and read
the new quiz.

Quiz: Do you know how to decode the personals?

**When writing an online personal ad, people are expected to describe
themselves fairly accurately. A little exaggeration is to be expected,
but one guy's "rugged" is often another guy's "acne-scarred."
How well do you know how to read the personals?**

1. He says he's "creative." This is code for:

    a ▶ Not good at sports

    b ▶ Mama's boy

    c ▶ Fashion victim

    d ▶ Criminally insane

    e ▶ All of the above

2. She says she's "voluptuous." That really means:

    a ▶ Sexy

    b ▶ Curvy

    c ▶ Busty

    d ▶ Has a huge butt

    e ▶ Fat

3. His face has "character." Translation?

    a ▶ His quirky personality is visible on his face

    b ▶ He's attractive in an unusual way

    c ▶ His looks aren't everybody's taste

    d ▶ He's hideous

4. He's taking a year off before college "to find himself." This means:

    a ▶ He's traveling the world

    b ▶ He's doing a lot of reading and deep thinking

    c ▶ He wasn't accepted anywhere

    d ▶ He's working at McDonald's

    e ▶ He's in jail

5. He's "looking for good times" or "just someone to hang with."
    In plain English:

    a ▶ He wants to take things slowly to make sure you're right
    for each other

    b ▶ He wants to be friends first

    c ▶ He's got a girlfriend

    d ▶ He wants sex and only sex, after which you will never hear
    from him again

6. She's looking for a "soul mate," meaning:

    a ▶ Someone who really understands her

    b ▶ Someone she has a lot of values in common with

    c ▶ Someone to have a lot of sex with

    d ▶ Someone who's not allergic to her cats

    e ▶ A sap who will do her bidding

    Answer Key: If you picked mostly d's and e's, you know your
    personals, probably from bitter experience. If you picked most-
    ly a's, b's, or c's, you're in for a shock.

"Another masterpiece," Lina said. "You're really good at
this, Holly." She glanced at the library bulletin board,
covered with notices and announcements. "Let's post a
notice on the board so everyone will know to check our
blog for the new quiz."

She typed up an announcement and printed it out.
Holly followed her to the bulletin board. While Holly

searched for an available thumbtack, Lina spotted something interesting.

"Hey, look at this." Lina pointed to a piece of paper tacked to the bulletin board. "'Ode to Madison Markowitz.'"

'By Paco,' Holly read. That guy who'd said the only girl he wanted was Mads.

Mads walked in and found Holly and Lina staring at the bulletin board. "What are you reading?" Mads asked.

"Oh, nothing. Just a tribute to your loveliness." Lina pointed to the poem, scribbled in green ink on a piece of notebook paper.

"Oh my god," Mads said. "It's for me? It's a poem about me?" She unpinned the poem and read it with shaking hands.

Ode to Madison Markowitz
By "Paco"

I'm in love with Madison
I'll take her to my pad-ison
Together we'll be bad-ison
Oh Madison, my Madison

Oh my pretty Markowitz
Your beauty makes me bark-owitz
I want to see you stark-owitz
Naked.
My Madison! My Markowitz!

"It sucks," Madison said.

"Well, it may not be Shakespeare," Lina said. "But the feeling behind it—" She stopped. There was no denying it, it sucked. "It's still exciting," she said. "Somebody is crazy about you! And he's declaring his love in public— right here on the library bulletin board!"

"What if it's a joke?" Madison said.

"Who would go to so much trouble just to play a joke on you?" Holly said. "I mean, rhyming and everything. He could have saved himself a lot of hassle by using free verse."

"I think it's very romantic," Lina said.

"Who do you think Paco is?" Mads said. Lina and Holly shrugged.

"Maybe it's time for you to find out," Holly said.

"But if Sean didn't write this, I don't care who did," Mads said.

"Mads, even if it's not Sean, it's a guy who likes you," Lina said. "And Sean might hear about it, or see you together—"

"Guys like girls that other guys like," Holly added. "They're like sheep that way."

"You're right," Mads said. "Maybe I should give this Paco a try. What's the worst that could happen?"

On this point, Holly and Lina kept their thoughts to themselves.

14 The Poetry Flows

HERE IS TODAY'S HOROSCOPE: CANCER: You are this close to going over the edge. Wave to me on the way down, will you?

L ina kind of wished "Paco" hadn't written that poem for Mads—it made her question the wisdom of her latest secret plan.

She hadn't meant to do it. But she was up late one night, and she found herself writing a poem. It was a good poem, too. Just as good as anything Ramona and her friends wrote. There was no reason why it shouldn't be published, and the best place for it was *Inchworm*.

There was an established submission procedure for *Inchworm*: You were supposed to leave your work in the box outside the journal's office. Lina had seen Dan empty the submission box several times before. He probably made comments on the submissions and passed them on to the editors, Carrie and Ramona.

But Lina's poem wasn't meant for their eyes. It was meant for Dan only. Surely he would see that as soon as he read it. He would also see Lina's literary genius, that her voice was a gift to the world of poetry. A gift he must help her nurture and grow. At first, student and teacher would be united only by their love of the written word. But gradually, as the student blossomed into an irresistible young poetess, he would realize that love had blossomed, too. A love that transcended the boundaries of age differences, school rules, parental horror, and political correctness. A love for the ages.

And this poem was the beginning of it all.

Pedantry
I stand before you, waiting,
lost
out of balance, like a
violet plucked from the dewy grass too
early.
Don't leave before the petals fall
a moment too soon or too late makes all the difference
now.

Lina reread the poem with satisfaction. She knew she had gone a little overboard on Dan—that was why she couldn't share her real feelings with her friends. Maybe it was okay for Mads to go crazy over Sean, but this was different, more dangerous. And Holly always seemed so levelheaded. It shamed Lina. She was reluctant to reveal how unsensible she could be.

She folded up the poem and sealed it in an envelope. On the envelope she wrote *To Dan Shulman. Inchworm Poetry Submission.* Then she dropped it in the box to await its fate.

hollygolitely: any responses to your personal ad yet, mads?
mad4u: not really. one girl wrote offering to make over my
      makeover. Sebastiano made kissing noises at me today.
      I guess he thinks my picture is funny.

Holly sat in her room Tuesday night, not doing her Modern World History homework. As good a time as any to take an IM break with Mads.

hollygolitely: basti likes to tease.
mad4u: A few boys sent jokey answers, but no serious ones.
      Unless you count paco.
hollygolitely: paco answered your ad?
mad4u: ya. Wants to go out with me.
hollygolitely: and?

mad4u: guess I will. it's time to find out who this sucker is.

flappie: hey holly, whatcha doing? It's me, Rob.

hollygolitely: mads, rob just im'ed me! I'll get back to you.

mad4u: right on.

hollygolitely: hi rob. Just goofing off. where'd you get your
      screen name?

flappie: stupid, isn't it? my dad calls me that when I make
      pancakes. Flapjacks. Cause I'm good at flipping them. I
      just didn't know what to pick for a screen name.

hollygolitely: I like it. Pancakes are a good thing.

flappie: so how's the ihd project going? any juicy stuff?

hollygolitely : plenty. Did you know there's a boy in our school
      whose most embarrassing moment was when his step-
      sister put permanent green dye in his bathing suit? He
      said he was green down there for weeks, and the guys
      on his swim team started calling him alien butt.

flappie: I think I know who that was. Is he a junior?

hollygolitely: yeah. But I think he'd like to remain anonymous.

flappie: Well, just wanted to check in. better get back to the
      civil war. Wait—one more thing. Do you have a date for
      the winter dance yet?

hollygolitely: no. do you?

flappie: no. want to be my date?

hollygolitely: ok. Sounds good.

flappie: great. We'll talk later.

hollygolitely: q-l. bye.

flappie: c-u.

Holly screamed with excitement. Rob asked her to the dance! It was a very good sign. Maybe her Boobmeister phase was coming to an end at last. Most boys didn't ask the school slut to a dance.

She logged off and tried to study her history textbook. World War I. Was she crazy? How could she study at a time like this? She logged back on and IM'ed Mads and Lina.

hollygolitely: stop what u'r doing right now. rob asked me to the winter dance!

linaonme: x-l-ent!

mad4u: u r so lucky

linaonme: bet jake will be jealous.

hollygolitely: guess what? I don't care!

mad4u: u r right. Rob's way cooler.

hollygolitely: mads, did u write paco yet?

mad4u: negatory.

linaonme: write him! maybe he can be YOUR date for the dance!

mad4u: what about u, lina?

linaonme: don't worry about me. I'll be fine.

To: paco
From: mad4u
Re: my ad

Okay. I give in. Who are you? I am ready to meet you and learn your identity.

To: Mad4u

From: paco

Re: excellent!

You have made me the happiest guy in the world! But you must be patient. Soon I will leave you a clue to my identity. Until then, truly it is I who is mad-4-u.

Mads slapped her keyboard in frustration. She couldn't believe it! He wouldn't tell her who he was? He was leaving her a clue? She wanted to know right then and there, so she could research him before she had to look him in the face. Make sure he was Mads material. Because she had a funny feeling that anybody who was this crazy about her had to have something wrong with him.

Dear Lina,

Thank you for your recent submission to Inchworm. *Unfortunately, your work does not suit our needs at this time. Please feel free to submit any other work you may have in the future.*

Sincerely,

The Editors

Inchworm, *The Literary Journal of RSAGE*

Lina's heart sank as she read the rejection letter. How

could they? At the very least her poem was no worse than the usual drivel they published. Did Ramona intercept the envelope and open it herself, even though it was addressed to Dan? Did Dan ever see the poem?

Underneath the printed letter was a hand-scrawled note.

Lina—Your poem isn't a total loss. We might reconsider it if you'd be willing to revise it. Carrie, Siobhan, and I thought your work was too flowery and suffered from a lack of rawness. You could try adding more religious and death imagery, such as rivers of blood, serpents, gates of hell, and ritual disembowelment. Or you could go in another direction completely. Here's one suggestion for how your poem might read:

Girl
I know what you've trying to do with your
Violets in the grass and
Everything but it's
Useless. Listen, I'm only trying to hell-
P

Of course, this only a suggestion—one editor's opinion—and you should feel free to stick to your own vision, however pathetic.

Ramona

p.s. The Dan Shulman Cult (DSC) meets every

Friday in our clubhouse (my room). We have a small museum of Dan memorabilia—used coffee cups, graded papers, and so on. You are cordially invited to attend the next meeting this Friday. I'll assume you don't have a date. —RF

Lina angrily crumpled up the note. Ramona thought she was so smart! It was obviously her one defense against being a total misfit loser.

Ramona couldn't stop Lina so easily. She might be able to intercept Dan's private mail at school, but she couldn't do it at home. Actually, Lina wouldn't put it past her—it would be just like Ramona to cast a spell on the U.S. Postal Service to make sure Lina's mail got lost.

Lina wouldn't take any chances. She'd deliver the poem to Dan herself. In person. By hand. Just to make sure he got it. And to keep Ramona out of it, she'd deliver it to him at home.

Lina told herself this was in the service of literary justice. All she wanted was for the faculty advisor of *Inchworm* to see her poem. For her poem to have a fair shot at publication. That's all. That was the only reason she was going to Dan's house. It made perfect sense to Lina. If she didn't think about it too hard.

15 Paco Revealed

To:	mad4u
From:	Your daily horoscope

HERE IS TODAY'S HOROSCOPE: VIRGO: You will confront an inscrutable mystery today. And that mystery is: What did you do to deserve this?

Madison,

The time has come at last. Meet me in the art room after school today and you will finally learn the true identity of the one who loves you more than beef burritos, cheez doodles, or life itself.

—paco

Thursday morning, 8:30 AM. Mads tore the note off her locker and read it again. The handwriting was boyish and messy—it didn't go with the flowery words at all. Maybe that was a good thing.

The day slogged by, each minute seeming to drag like an hour. Geometry, Mads' most hated and tortured subject, was last period that day. Ms. Mildred Weymouth, her Geometry teacher, was a stout, perfectly nice lady in her sixties with a glass eye and a voice that could put a hyperactive kid into a coma. That was why they called her "Sleep-eez," when they didn't call her "Mildew."

At last, at last, the final bell rang. Mads dumped her books in her locker and checked her face and hair in the mirror she kept taped inside the door. She'd decided to go easy on the makeup, since some of the kids were calling her "raccoon eyes" after they saw her personal ad photo.

Okay. Time to meet her fate.

She walked up to the third floor. The art room was lodged in an attic space on top of the school, with skylights and windows that looked out over the town.

Mads stopped in front of the door and took a deep breath. *Please, Paco, be someone cool,* she prayed. She opened the door and stepped into the room. It was empty, except for lots of artwork, obviously, and Yucky Gilbert.

What was he doing there? Paco would be there any minute now, and she didn't want Gilbert around yucking things up.

"Hi, Madison," Gilbert said.

"Hi, Gilbert," Mads said. "What are you doing here? I'm meeting someone."

"I know," Gilbert said. "You're meeting me."

Again? Mads' brain fought against the obvious conclusion. The last person she wanted to see was Gilbert. She was most emphatically *not* there to meet him. But her heart sank as she realized that *he* was there to see *her*. Again.

He stood up and walked slowly toward her, dressed in a pair of brown plaid pants that were too small for him. His long legs poked out of the pants like toothpicks.

"I'm 'Paco,'" Gilbert explained.

Mads clutched at a chair and sat down. "No," she gasped. "You can't be Paco. You already filled out a questionnaire. You're 'John'!"

"I'm Paco *and* John," Gilbert said. "I filled out two questionnaires, using different screen names. I wanted to make sure I was matched up with you somehow. I figured if I put my name in the hat twice, it would double my chances. Are you surprised?"

Damn right she was surprised. It had never occurred to her that Gilbert would use two different names. She thought she'd disposed of him when she got rid of "John." Now it turned out he was like a self-replicating mutant, or a robot who multiplies and comes back stronger every time you try to destroy it.

"That's not fair," she managed to say. Her throat felt

tight. She was so disappointed. "You'll ruin the results of our IHD project."

"I don't care," Gilbert said. "I'm ruthless. I'll do anything to get you."

He pulled a bunch of roses wrapped in cellophane from behind his back and presented them to her. She gripped the stems with her cold, cold fingers.

"Madison, I have something very important to talk about with you," Gilbert said. "I have a confession to make. It's a little embarrassing, but I know I can trust you."

"What is it?" Mads asked. She wanted desperately to leave but her legs felt frozen stiff.

"Madison, I'm a virgin." Mads looked up at him. Did she hear him right? Or was this all just part of some terrible dream?

"Did you just say you were a virgin?" Mads asked. "At twelve? Gee, that's a shocker."

"Yes, it's true," Gilbert said, wiping his nose with his sleeve. "I know it's hard to believe. But I have decided to lose my virginity with you. You're a little older than I am, so you must be more advanced, right?"

Oh my god, Mads thought. If only he knew. Was Gilbert sent by the devil to torture her?

"So is it a deal?" Gilbert asked. "Can we do it as soon as possible? We could lock the art room door and do it right here, right now. What do you say?"

Gilbert flashed her a big smile and got down in front of her on one knee, arms open wide.

Mads stared at him in disbelief. The roses fell from her hands to the floor, but she didn't notice or care. She was too stunned to speak.

Gilbert's smile faded, but he wasn't giving up hope yet. "Or I could take you out on a date first," he offered. "That would be fine, too."

Slowly, the icy shock that had held her in its grip began to thaw. Mads wiggled her fingers and toes. She wanted to run screaming from the room, but she wasn't sure her legs would hold her up.

She slowly got to her feet, testing her strength. "I understand your situation, Gilbert," she said in a calm voice. "Believe me, I feel for you. But I can't help you. I'm sorry, but I'm not interested."

Gilbert shuffled across the floor on his knees in a panic. "Madison, if you'd give me a chance to win you over—"

Madison's calm, polite shell cracked. It had never been too sturdy to begin with. Her legs, however, were fine.

"No!" she shouted. "Get away from me!"

Now she ran screaming from the room.

"Madison, come back!" Gilbert shouted. "Will you go to the dance with me?"

16 The Dance Begins

| To: | mad4u, hollygolitely, linaonme |
| From: | Your daily horoscope |

HERE IS TODAY'S HOROSCOPE: SOLAR ECLIPSE! Another huge astrological event. Unfortunately, it will happen in the Southern Hemisphere, so you Northerners won't get to see it. But that doesn't mean it won't affect you. The stars predict close encounters, close calls, and close shaves for everybody.

I'll meet you girls back here at eleven, all right?" Lina's father said to Lina and Mads, leaning out the window of his black Lexus sedan.

"All right, Dad. Thanks," Lina said.

"Thanks, Mr. Ozu," Mads said. It had only been a few joyous weeks since Holly got her driver's license, but Lina and Mads were already used to having her pick them up for parties and stuff. It felt like a hardship to have to rely on a parent again.

"What if Holly and Rob become a couple?" Mads asked. "Holly will never want to drive us anywhere. And you're not turning sixteen until July!"

"But if Holly likes Rob . . . " Lina said. "I mean, I don't think that's a very good reason to want them not to get together."

"I know. It's totally selfish and I'm a terrible person. We'll just have to cozy up to Rebecca or somebody. I think her birthday's in March."

They stood outside the school entrance, watching the students pour in for the dance. Then they went inside and down the hall to the auditorium, which had been lamely decorated with fake snow, an igloo, and colored lights. There was no band, just a DJ—somebody's older brother—hired by the social committee. Still, even though they pretended it was no big deal, Lina and Mads were excited. Mads hoped Sean would be there. Maybe she could dance near him and he'd turn around and they'd dance together, even if only for a few seconds.

Lina had borrowed her mother's perfume, just in case Dan somehow stood close to her. Maybe he'd catch a whiff of the sophisticated scent and it would stay with him, haunting him, making him think of Lina in a new way. . . .

"Hi, girls." There he was. Dan stood by the door, welcoming the kids as they entered the auditorium. He wore his usual suit and skinny tie, dressed up with a porkpie hat. "You both look great."

Lina felt her face flame. She knew he was saying it in a general way to both her and Mads. But still his words had an effect on her—she couldn't help it.

"Thanks," she said.

"Have a good time tonight," he said. The girls walked in. He stayed at the door to greet more kids. Music was blasting but nobody was dancing yet.

"Let's get a drink," Mads said, and they made a beeline for the soda table. It was something to do. They got sodas and leaned against a wall, watching and waiting to see how the chips would fall as the kids settled in.

Lina's eyes kept wandering back to Dan at the door. How did he treat everyone? Pretty evenly, it seemed. But he must like some students more than others, must have some secret signal he gives out to show it, even if he isn't aware of it. . . . Ugh, in came Ramona, with Siobhan, Chandra, and Maggie. They were in full vampire makeup, black hair streaked with temporary red stripes, towering black lace-up boots and gauzy Stevie Nicks dresses. They fluttered around Dan like moths, pretending to cast some kind of witchy spell on him. He laughed and played along. Just being nice, probably. Then they scurried out to the dance floor, the first ones to start dancing, all together in a circle, twirling and spinning as if caught up in some kind of secret ecstasy. God, they bugged Lina. They acted as if they knew something no one else did, as if they had a secret wisdom or knowledge. But Lina suspected—no, knew—it was just an act, a way to make themselves feel special. Underneath the costumes and hair dye and cakey makeup they were just regular doofuses like everybody else.

"Hey." Mads nudged her. "There's Holly and Rob."

Holly looked so pretty in her form-fitting knit dress and knee-high boots, her heavy hair piled up messily on top of her head, that Mads regretted her selfish tantrum about driving.

Holly waved and left Rob for a minute to greet them. "You guys look so cute!" she said.

"How's it going?" Lina asked, meaning the date with Rob.

"No glitches yet," Holly said. "We just got here. If somebody besides the four witches would dance, maybe we would, too. You should come dance with us!"

"No," Mads said. "This is like a first date for you. We'll wait until you're a well-established couple, then we'll barge in on you."

"Don't worry about us," Lina said. "Go!"

Holly glowed. She trotted back to Rob. They went to the drink table for sodas.

Lina and Mads checked out the chaperones, clustered in two clumps near the door and the drink table. "There's Mildew," Mads said, "the snooze machine. Look what she's wearing."

The stout Ms. Weymouth wore a bright-orange flowered caftan and a lei made of plastic flowers. She was droning in the ear of Frank Welling, the art teacher, who was dressed according to theme in a puffy ski outfit.

"What do you think they're talking about?" Mads said. Ms. Weymouth and Mr. Welling seemed to have nothing in common—except, of course, that they both taught at Rosewood. And their last names started with W.

"Maybe she's flirting with him," Lina said. "Or trying to pick him up! Like, 'Oh, Frank, meet me in the woods behind the gym. Make passionate love to me, Frank!'"

Mads laughed. "Yeah, and he's saying, 'Will do, Mildew. Just give me a few minutes to shoot myself in the head first.' Isn't she married?"

"I don't know. Probably."

"It's funny that the chaperones don't bring dates to the dance," Mads said. "You know, so they'd have somebody to dance with."

"I don't see why they can't dance with students," Lina said.

"I bet you don't," Mads said.

Mademoiselle Barker, a slender, pretty young French

teacher with sleek, short dark hair and a fringe along her forehead too short to call bangs, twirled across the room to the door and started talking to Dan. She took his hand and danced a few steps in front of him, hips swaying, while he stood rooted in place and laughed.

She's not married, Lina thought. *If she were, we'd call her Madame.*

Mlle. Barker did another skirt-flying spin and gave up on Dan for the moment. A new song played and a group of football players stormed the dance floor, stomping their feet and clapping. Must have been some anthem they warmed up to in the locker room before games.

Mads suddenly pinched Lina's upper arm, then tightened her grip. "Sean's here," she whispered.

"Ow." Lina yanked her arm away. Sean walked in with his friends Alex Sipress, Barton Mitchell, and Mo Basri. Sean had his arm around a pretty girl Lina didn't recognize. She was tall and blond with long bangs that nearly hid her large, black-lined eyes. She was wearing jeans and boots and a too-small military jacket over a tight t-shirt. She looked as if she hadn't planned on going to a dance at all, which of course made her the hippest girl in the room. She was too cool to go to a school dance; this was just a lark for her, on the way to bigger and better things.

"Who's that?" Mads asked.

"Maybe it's Sean's sister," Lina said.

"Sean doesn't have a sister," Mads said. "And don't say cousin. She's obviously not his cousin either."

Sean swung the girl around until she was dizzy, then pulled her tightly against him and kissed her on the mouth.

"Guess she goes to another school," Lina said. Or college. The girl had to be at least eighteen.

Mads stared at them, scowling. How could she ever compete with a girl like that? No matter what Mads did, no matter how sophisticated she tried to be, she'd never be that cool. It was like trying to compete with a movie star—so impossible, so depressing, Mads couldn't even hold the thought in her mind. She let it fly away and returned to her usual state of ditzy optimism.

"So Sean has a date," Mads said. "It's not as if I didn't expect it. I'm in this for the long haul." She aimed her laser vision at Sean's friends: Alex, Barton, and Mo.

"Alex is the cutest," Lina said.

"I concur," Mads said. "Alex it is. I'll hook up with Sean's friend. He'll have to notice that. It may take some time to maneuver from Alex to Sean, but at least step one will be accomplished: Sean will realize that I am not a little kid. If I'm mature enough to be with his friend Alex, then I'm mature enough to be with him."

Mads presented herself to Lina for inspection. Everything checked out okay. "Go get him," Lina said.

"Hey, Lina." Walker slouched up to her in his cool-guy way. "Want to dance?"

Lina glanced at Mads, who practically pushed her onto the dance floor. "Mads, why don't you dance with us?" Lina said.

"Yeah, Mads," Walker said, taking both girls' hands and leading them onto the floor. "Come on. I love this song."

The three of them danced together to OutKast. Mads maneuvered their group to be near Sean. The dance floor was crowded now, everybody dancing whether they had a partner or not, but Sean was definitely dancing with the blond girl.

Mads turned away from Lina and found herself face-to-face with Alex. He grinned, grabbed her hand, and twirled her around. Mads laughed, delighted. The OutKast song segued into the Neptunes, and Alex didn't let Mads go. Mads did her sexy shimmy, and Alex laughed.

They kept going, song after song, until Mads didn't know where Holly or Lina were, or even Sean. She and Alex were in their own little dance world, hot and sweaty. Just as Mads was getting thirsty and thinking of stopping for a drink, a pale face framed by a pageboy haircut popped into her field of vision. Yucky Gilbert.

"Aauugh!" Mads screamed.

"Hi, Madison!" Gilbert was looking his yuckiest in a pea-green knit shirt that emphasized his sallow skin tone.

Alex elbowed Gilbert away. "Dude, we're dancing here." Thank god for Alex. Mads thought she could fall in love with him for that gesture alone.

She danced on, afraid to stop for a drink now. It might give Gilbert an opening and Alex a chance to leave. She tried to shut Gilbert out, but he kept buzzing around her, arms and legs flailing. One of his arms flew up and accidentally slapped the back of her head.

"Ow!" Mads cried, rubbing her head.

"Do you know this guy?" Alex asked.

"Not really," Mads said. "Gilbert, leave us alone!"

"May I cut in?" he asked, so beyond getting the hint that a steamroller couldn't have stopped him. He placed himself between Mads and Alex and let his arms and legs flap around like noodles.

Mads gave up. "Want to get something to drink?" she asked Alex.

"Yeah."

They walked away, leaving Gilbert dancing by himself for a few seconds. When he realized he'd been abandoned, he followed them to the drink table. He took a flask from his jacket pocket and waved it under Mads' nose. "Irish up your Sprite, Mads?" he offered, unscrewing the top of the flask. "I've got melon liqueur in here. I wanted vodka but my mom only drinks melon liqueur. She puts it in her diet smoothies."

"No, thanks." Alex's eyes were scanning the room. His attention was straying. No! She had to keep him interested. She had to get rid of Gilbert.

At the other end of the auditorium, Mr. Welling and some social committee kids were setting up a pizza table. A long line of kids had already formed, waiting for slices.

"Why don't you go get us some pizza, Gilbert?" Mads asked. That ought to keep him busy for a while. The line was growing fast. Maybe she and Alex could slip away before he came back.

"Okay, Madison," Gilbert said. "Whatever you like. Hey, they've got garlic knots. Do you like garlic knots?"

"Sure, whatever," Mads said. "Just hurry up and get in line before it gets too long."

Gilbert bounded away. Mads breathed a sigh of relief. He turned and waved at her from the end of the line.

Alex touched Mads' back. She took that as an encouraging sign.

"Can we get out of here for a little while?" Mads asked.

"Sure," Alex said. "Let's go out to my car."

"Perfect." Gilbert would never find them there. Well, knowing Gilbert, he might, but at least it would take a while.

She and Alex left the auditorium. Lina saw them slip away. She checked on Holly and Rob, still dancing like crazy. Lina wished she felt more like dancing. But it was hard to have fun at a dance when your friends were preoccupied and the one you love was so near but still out of reach.

"Feel like some pizza?" Walker asked her.

"No, thanks," Lina said. Walker was nice, she knew that. But somehow she just couldn't manage to focus on him. She danced with him, she listened to him talk, but she kept half an eye on Dan. She watched Dan carry a stack of empty pizza boxes to the trash. She turned her attention back to the dance floor. All those squirming bodies, the flashing lights, the loud music, suddenly made her feel dizzy and disoriented.

"I have to go to the bathroom," she told Walker. "I'll be back in a minute."

She slipped out and stood in the silent hallway, leaning against the cool tile wall. What was wrong with her? Why couldn't she just let go and have a good time?

The auditorium door pushed open, and a blast of noise rushed out into the hall and hushed again as the door swung shut. Lina glanced over. Dan stepped out, saw her, and smiled.

"Hey," he said, walking over to her. He leaned against the wall as she did, patting a pocket in his jacket. "Thought I might sneak out for a smoke, but I guess you caught me."

"I won't tell anyone," Lina said. At the sight of him her heart started racing and her mind fogged. She struggled to keep it clear so she wouldn't say anything stupid.

"What are you doing out here?" Dan asked. "I saw you dancing earlier. Looked like you were having fun."

"Not really," Lina said. "I mean, yeah. I don't know. I just needed to take a break."

"I know what you mean." He pulled a cigarette from his pocket, rolled it between his fingers, and put it back. "I hated dances when I was in high school. I always felt like such a dork. I couldn't dance at all. Still can't."

Lina smiled, but she couldn't help wondering in alarm if he thought she was a dork too. Maybe he liked dorks. *No, don't be stupid,* she told herself. *Nobody likes dorks.*

"I guess I'm just not in the mood for a dance tonight," she said. "I didn't know you smoked."

"Every once in a while," he said. "I don't know, maybe it's just an excuse to get out of there for a few minutes." He gave a small, conspiratorial laugh, as if the two of them were in this together, refugees from the dance from hell. That little laugh made Lina so happy she wanted to throw her head back and yelp.

A shriek and high-pitched giggling echoed down the hallway. Autumn, Rebecca, and Claire were on their way back from the bathroom. They dropped their voices and glanced at Lina and Dan as they skipped past them and burst through the auditorium doors. The music blared and faded again.

"Well, guess I better get back in there," Dan said. "Maybe I'll skip the smoke. Don't want to get into trouble."

"Okay." Lina didn't know what else to say. She tried to come up with something witty or profound but her mind let her down as usual. She pressed the toe of her boot into the buffed, shiny floor.

"But you're all right, right?" Dan asked, pushing away from the wall. "I mean, nothing's wrong, is it?"

"No!" Lina shook her head with too much animation. "I'm fine. Really. I was just about to go back inside, too. I was just, you know, standing here for a minute. . . ."

"Okay. Good. Well, see you in there." Dan tipped the rim of his porkpie hat to her and went back to the dance. Lina closed her eyes and pressed the back of her head against the wall. Oh my god. How could he be so charming? It was killing her!

She wished Mads would come back. She had to tell somebody about what had just happened. She needed to analyze every detail of this encounter, the meaning of every word and gesture. He was worried about her! He wanted to make sure he was okay! It was amazing!

Was he flirting with her? Was he sending her a signal? Lina still couldn't believe he had even noticed her enough to be concerned. Maybe he'd been watching her all night! He said he was watching her dance! Oh my god! Lina could hardly contain herself. She didn't see how she could go back in there and keep up the charade of polite interest with Walker now. But what else could she do? She ran down the hall to the bathroom. Then she ran back to the auditorium. She was going to grab Holly, just for a few minutes, and drag her into the bathroom with her. She had to tell somebody!

"Hey, Safran, having a good time?" Jake, trailed by two of his soccer buddies and a couple of girls, found Holly and Rob perched on the lip of the stage. They were taking a break, drinking sodas, watching the dancers.

"'Cause if you're not having fun now, you will later," Jake said in an obnoxious, insinuating tone. "Am I right? Huh?"

Just the sight of Jake left a sour taste in Holly's mouth. How could she ever have liked him? He was such a thug!

"How would you know, Jake?" Holly snapped. "Your idea of a good time is sitting home kissing your pillow."

"You had a pretty good time with me a couple of weeks ago," Jake said. "You couldn't get enough."

Holly couldn't believe his nerve, lying right to her face! When he knew that she knew the truth. He must have thought she'd be too intimidated to contradict him. He thought wrong.

"Funny, Jake, I don't remember that," Holly said. "But then, it's hard for me to know what you see *in your dreams!*"

"Zing!" someone shouted.

Rob took Holly's hand and led her away. "Come on," he said. "Before you two start scratching each other's eyes out."

"That ought to shut him up," Holly muttered. She forgot all about her Boobmeister rep when she was with Rob—and then Jake had to throw it back in her face. And in Rob's face. She wondered what Rob really thought of her. Did he believe her—or did he believe Jake?

"Holly!" Lina ran up to them, her eyes shining. "Come to the bathroom with me."

Holly glanced at Rob. Obviously Lina had something to share that was not for male ears.

"Go," Rob said. "Before Jake comes around asking for more punishment."

Lina looked confused, so Holly said, "I'll tell you mine after you tell me yours."

"Deal."

"Where'd you learn to dance like that?" Alex asked. Mads sat with him in the front seat of his Toyota. He was holding her hand and rubbing it gently with his thumb.

"Do you like it?" Mads asked. "Or do you think it's goofy?" Mads knew her dancing style could be a little over-the-top, but she wasn't bad at it. She could dislocate the different parts of her body like a belly dancer, and knew how to wiggle her hips in a sexy way that was also kind of funny.

"Sure I like it," Alex said. "It's hot."

All right. This was going great. "I took ballet and stuff when I was younger," Mads said. "Some modern dance. You learn how to move all the parts of your body in different ways."

She leaned closer now, parting her lips and putting them in kissing range. He took the bait. He pulled her head toward his and pressed his mouth against hers. She opened her mouth and his tongue wiggled in. Wow. He was a good kisser.

"Mmm," he said. She put her arms around his neck and pulled her body closer. He put his arms around her and pressed her against him. He had strong arms.

He came up for air, kissed her neck, and murmured, "Hey, Madison, you sure are sweet. . . ."

They kissed again, really getting into it. *This is it,* Mads thought. *I'm finally getting some experience—with Sean's friend Alex! It's not Sean, but it's close.*

He rubbed her back and started inching his hand toward her chest. Mads heard a sound, a knocking sound. She ignored it, and Alex didn't seem to hear it either. But then it came again, knuckle on glass, louder this time. Oh no. Someone was knocking on the window. *Please don't let it be Gilbert,* Mads prayed.

That prayer, at least, was answered.

"Hey, Alex!" It was Sean. "Open up! Don't steam up the windows too much!"

Mads and Alex broke apart. Alex rolled down the window. "Hey, man, what are you doing in there?" Sean asked. He was with the blond girl and Barton and Mo. He nodded at Mads. "Hey, kid."

He noticed her!

"Nothing," Alex said. "What's up?"

"Jane wants to leave, and I'm starving," Sean said. "They've got nothing to eat here but that lame pizza. Let's go get a burger or something."

"All right," Alex said. Sean and the others opened the car doors and started piling in.

Mads couldn't believe it. "You're hungry?"

"Yeah. Aren't you?"

Food was the last thing on her mind. She climbed out of the car to straighten her clothes. Mo jumped into the front seat. There was no room left in the car for her.

"Do you want to come with us?" Alex asked, starting the car.

Mads looked for a spot in the car, but it was full. The only way she'd fit was if she sat on someone's lap. And no one offered.

"Thanks anyway," she said.

"Okay. Well, see you around."

Sean sat in the backseat with his arm draped over Jane's shoulders. "Hey, kid, see you at my party next Saturday, all right?"

Party? He was inviting her to a party? At his very own house?

"Sure, see you then!" she called.

Alex drove away, music blaring, leaving Mads to go back to the dance alone.

Had Alex just dumped her for a hamburger? She knew boys were always hungry but this was ridiculous.

She thought of the Dating Game and their IHD thesis. What had made them think that boys were more sex-crazed than girls? She couldn't imagine herself ever turning away from a boy she liked just to get some food. Well, maybe for her dad's homemade strawberry ice cream . . . no, not even for that. Anyway, she'd share it with the boy.

Who cared about Alex anyway? Sean himself had invited *her*, Madison Markowitz, tenth grader, to his party next Saturday night. He actually wanted her to be there! She was making progress! Her plan was working!

She found Gilbert waiting faithfully for her in the auditorium. He was holding two plates, one with a slice of pizza and one with a pile of little salty rolls. He offered her a plate. "Garlic knot?"

17 The Velvet Clown Painting

To:	linaonme
From:	Your daily horoscope

HERE IS TODAY'S HOROSCOPE: CANCER: You're feeling brave and bold. You're capable of anything right now. That's what everyone is afraid of.

Lina stared at the inkblot test they used on the Dating Game site. What did it look like to her? A pizza crust with teethmarks on it. Was that the answer of a sex-crazed person? It might not seem so at first, but Lina would have to say yes.

At the dance she saw Ramona take a leftover pizza crust off Dan's plate after he dropped it in the trash. She couldn't get the image out of her mind—the bitten pizza crust, his teethmarks and the little bits of tomato sauce left on it . . . Ramona had slipped it into her purse. What could the Dan Shulman Cult possibly do with it? And yet, deep down, she understood why they'd want it. Ugh, she was so pathetic!

She still had the poem she'd written, "Pedantry." She was working up the courage to deliver it to him. At his house. If, as a bonus, her insatiable curiosity about what the inside of his house looked like was satisfied, well, that was incidental.

It was Saturday, the day after the dance. She sealed the poem in an envelope, got on her bike, and rode toward school. Dan lived a mile or two past the school in an old residential area lined with small bungalows. She'd ridden her bike through there before, just checking things out. She knew Dan's address by heart—it was printed in the school directory.

She stopped in front of his house, a tiny, one-story, pale green cottage set in a small cluster of trees. She strad-dled her bike and took it in. A cracked cement walk led to the front door, which was framed by shrubs on both sides. A beat-up old Honda sat in the driveway under a carport awning. There wasn't a garage.

Lina was suddenly paralyzed with anxiety. What would he do when he saw her? What would she say? Oh my god, what if someone was there with him? One of his friends? Or a girl? Or his mother? Did he live with someone? Why did her brain have to wait until this moment to think of that?

Maybe he wouldn't be home, and she could just slip the poem under his door or leave it in the mailbox. Part of her desperately wished for him to be out, but a stronger part wanted to see him, to test his reaction to her.

She walked her bike up to the door and leaned it against the black iron rail that marked the four front steps. In her mind she practiced what to say. *Hi, Dan, I was just riding my bike around and . . . Hello, surprised to see me? . . . Uh, Dan, did you realize you're the object of a goth-girl cult which at this very moment is probably trying to cast a love spell on you using a discarded pizza crust? Just thought I'd give you a heads-up . . .* Ugh, nothing seemed right!

She took a deep breath and rang the doorbell. She waited and listened. She heard a chair scrape across a floor. Someone was definitely home.

The door opened and there he stood. Dressed for a Saturday in old-man slacks and a button-down thrift-store shirt. He really was committed to his style.

"Lina!" He sounded surprised, and why wouldn't he be? "What are you doing here? Is everything okay?"

"Hi, Dan. Everything's fine. I—uh—"

"Here, come on in." He stepped aside and opened the door wider so she could come in. She couldn't believe she was about to step into his house. She put her foot on the little rag rug in the doorway. Another step and she stood on the wooden floor of the tiny entrance. A kitchen with a breakfast bar was just to the right, and beyond that a small living room/dining room. She couldn't get much sense of the furniture, other than the velvet paint-by-numbers clown that hung over a rickety red table in the hall.

A pained look—fear, consternation, regret, Lina wasn't sure—crossed Dan's face suddenly, as if he'd realized he'd just made a mistake. "So, what brings you here?" he asked again.

"I wanted to give you this." Lina handed him the envelope, carefully sealed with *Dan Shulman* written in her best handwriting on the front. He took it and stared at it.

"Oh, okay. Thanks."

"It's a poem," Lina explained. "For *Inchworm*. I wanted to make sure you had a chance to read it. I don't trust those school mailboxes, you know, anybody can go through them and read anything you put in there—"

"Yeah, you're right, no security at that school," Dan said. "Well, Lina, it sure is nice to see you. I'll read this right away and let you know what I think when I see you at school on Monday. Okay?"

He seemed in a big hurry to get her out of the house. She peered over his shoulder in search of a sign that someone was there, but she didn't sense the presence of another person. *Duh*, she thought, finally realizing what was bothering him. *He's afraid to have a student alone with him in his house! Especially a girl student! Even more especially a girl student he likes,* she convinced herself.

"So, again, I promise I'll read this and I won't show it to anyone else unless you say it's okay." Dan moved his hands toward her shoulders as if he were going to gently move her toward the door, then suddenly stopped as if he'd thought better of it. He rubbed his head instead. A bead of sweat had popped up on his hairline.

Lina didn't want to leave, but she knew she should let him off the hook. "Thank you, Dan."

"Come see me on Monday," he said. "And we'll talk about it."

"Okay." She went out and picked up her bike. "Bye."

"Bye." He watched her all the way down the walk, watched her get on her bike and waved as she pedaled away. When she glanced back he was gone and the door was closed.

He was nervous, she thought. That could be good or bad or have nothing to do with her. She decided to consider it good. And what would he think after he read her poem? If he wanted her to make the next move, the poem was it.

All right, Dan, she thought. *The ball's in your court now.*

18 Sex Tips for Girls

To:	linaonme
From:	Your daily horoscope

HERE IS TODAY'S HOROSCOPE: CANCER: Today doesn't look too bad, Cancer, as long as you don't mind a little pain, and maybe some heartbreak to go along with it.

Hey, look," Lina called from her desk, where she was sorting the latest Dating Game questionnaires and making matches. "Autumn wants us to match her with somebody!"

"Let's put her with Gilbert," Mads said. "He needs someone to take his mind off me."

"I'm sorry, Mads, but I can't do that," Lina said. "It goes against the Matchmaker's Code. 'First, do no harm.'"

"That's impossible," Mads said. "Harm happens. Risk

is built into the whole idea of matchmaking. That's the fun of it."

Lina, Holly, and Mads sat in Lina's big bedroom, with its reading nook and white carpet and windows looking out over the bay. Lina's room had its own bathroom and even a sliding door that led to a private little patio. Her house was elegant. That's what Mads thought, anyway. No pesky brothers or sisters. So clean and animal-free. Surrounded by trees on three sides, overlooking the water in the back, it was a sleek modern house made of blond wood and glass, all on one level but much larger than it looked.

"If there's a Matchmaker's Code, there ought to be a Blogger's Code, too," Holly said. "No spreading lies about your classmates on your blog, Miss Nuclear Autumn. She deserves whatever creep she gets. Try Jake."

"Come on, just one date with Gilbert ought to cure her," Mads said.

"Gilbert won't go out with her, and you know it," Lina said. "He loves you and only you."

"Lucky me. Gilbert likes me because he's the only person in school who has less of a love life than I have."

"Stop exaggerating, Mads," Holly said. "You're too obsessed with this experience thing. What's the big deal? Some people have fooled around more than other people. So what?"

"That's easy for you to say," Mads said. "You're the

Boobmeister. No one ever refuses to go out with you because you're too young. My self-esteem is taking a beating here. I put myself out there, I try to sex up my image, and I get nothing. Guys would rather have a snack than make out with me. Thank god Sean invited me to his party! If he hadn't, I might be hurting right now."

She opened a container of vanilla yogurt and spooned some into her mouth. "I wonder what we'll talk about at Sean's party," she said.

"Oh, it will be deep," Holly said. "Sean and his friends are probably *this close* to discovering an alternative energy source." She paused and added, "I wonder if Rob will ask me to go to the party with him."

After the dance Friday night they drove to Harvey's Carry-Out for milkshakes, and then Rob dropped her off at home. They kissed good-night but didn't fool around or anything. It was late, anyway, but Holly wondered if Jake's teasing had turned Rob off or freaked him out somehow. Or maybe he was just waiting for a better time to pounce on her.

Holly reached for a *Cosmo* lying on the floor near Lina's bed. The cover promised to reveal "How to Drive a Guy Wild."

"Ooh, I read that," Mads said when she saw the magazine in Holly's hand. She plopped onto the bed beside Holly, and Lina sat down, too. "There's some weird stuff in there. Look at this one—'Grow your fingernails long and trail them down his back in sexy swirls.' I don't know, boys always seem to be too much in a hurry for that kind of thing."

"Maybe when they're older they're not so rushed," Lina said.

"'Put chocolate or whipped cream all over your body and let him lick it off,'" Holly read. "That would be pretty messy in a car."

Mads laughed. "There's that food thing again. They should recommend putting hamburger patties all over your body and letting them use you as a plate."

"'Feet are sexy,'" Lina read. "'Lie with your feet near his head and let him lick your toes.'"

"Look at these Kissing Tips," Mads said. "'Run your tongue along his teeth. Try nibbling on his lips to really make him go wild.'"

"Nibble on his lips?" Lina said. "Do you really think that works?"

Mads shrugged. "Who knows?"

"I don't think I'd want someone nibbling on my lips," Lina said. "There's something rabbity about it. But I guess if it was the right guy, I wouldn't mind."

She couldn't keep herself from imagining Dan nibbling on her lips, but the image was too potent for her and she quickly snuffed it out with a piece of chocolate. He must have read her poem by now. What did he think of it? More important, what would he do about it?

"So. About your poem."

Lina sat in the *Inchworm* office on the other side of the desk from Dan. He had her poem in front of him. Her sweaty right hand clutched at her sweaty left hand, but they were both so wet they slipped and slid between her fingers like clay.

"It—it's a good poem," Dan said. Lina waited for more, but he just stared at the poem and didn't look up and didn't say anything. So she said, "Thank you."

"I'd really love to publish your work in *Inchworm*," Dan said. "I'm sure Carrie and Ramona and the other editors would agree."

Ha, Lina thought.

"But I haven't shown them this poem, and I'm not going to. I think you understand why. Um, if we published this, it might cause a lot of, um, talk, and um, that's not really what you want, is it?"

He was as nervous as she was, that was clear. But what did it mean? Lina felt a surge of confidence. She had the power to make him nervous!

But she realized, if she was really being honest with herself, that she hadn't written the poem with publication in mind. She'd written it for him, and only for him. How extremely wise of him to understand that.

"No," she said. "I don't want to cause anyone any trouble, if that's what you mean."

His face cracked into an uncomfortable grin. "Right. So, I'll give this back to you, for you to keep." He handed her the poem. "You're a good writer, Lina, it's not that. But, um, I guess, you know, this should probably stay just between us."

She took the poem back. On the bottom of the page, in his red grading pen, Dan had started to write a note to her. *Dear Lina,* it said, but then he'd scratched it out.

Dear Lina. Was he just using the conventional letter greeting? Or was she really dear to him?

"So, you keep that, and write more poems!" Dan said. "Only, um, not about me. I mean, you can write about anything you want, freedom of speech and all that, but you, you know, probably shouldn't use my, um, name."

So he understood. She knew it was really kind of obvious, the device she'd used, where the first letter of every line spelled out "I love Dan." But it could be any Dan. Dan Morgenstern, the senior class president. Danny Dortmunder, a nondescript dweeb in her class. Danny DeVito, even, although that was a long shot. But, no. He knew who she meant. Dan Shulman. The one and only true Dan.

"I understand." She stood up to go.

"Good. Good. I'm glad." He seemed relieved. "Okay. So, everything's all right then?"

"Uh-huh."

"And, um, we understand each other?"

"Yes, I think so."

"Good. All right. See you later, Lina."

She left, the poem rattling in her trembling hands. Now she understood. Of course. This was dangerous for him. He couldn't admit his feelings for her openly. He liked her. She was pretty sure he liked her. But he couldn't come out and say it. So he tiptoed around it. He used euphemisms like "I think you're a good writer" and "This is just between us." Just between us, like two lovers with a secret!

So that was the way it would stay, a secret, for as long as she could stand it.

19 What Color Is His Toothbrush?

| To: | mad4u |
| From: | Your daily horoscope |

HERE IS TODAY'S HOROSCOPE: VIRGO: People will find you intoxicating today. Time to sober them up.

Are you sure I don't look too kooky?" Mads asked as she climbed out of the yellow VW. Saturday night and Sean's big Victorian house was already hopping, lights blazing, cars lining the street, kids stumbling across the lawn. From the sheer number of kids and the loudness of the music, Mads knew Sean's parents had to be away for the weekend.

Mads was dressed for the party in red high-heeled pumps, her lowest-riding jeans, and a stretchy red wrap top. Nothing weird about that; Holly was similarly dressed in boots, jeans, and a zip-up sweater. Lina wore a mod orange thrift-store mini dress, which drove her mother crazy. Sylvia didn't believe in wearing other people's used clothes.

It wasn't her clothes Mads was worried about, but her hair. To jazz up her look Mads had tried once more—or rather, let Audrey try—to give her fine hair a little volume. It puffed around her head like a black cloud.

"You look really cute," Lina said. Mads frowned. Cute was too easy for her. "I mean hot," Lina said. "You look hot."

Mads glanced at Holly for confirmation. "Hot," Holly reiterated. And she did look hot, except for the hair. Holly got her brush out of her purse and tried to mat Mads' hair down a little.

"Sean's tongue will be hanging to the floor when he sees you," Lina said.

The house sat on top of a small hill. They climbed the stairs to the front porch, where about six kids were lounging around. Holly scanned the group for Rob, but he wasn't there. Mads had begged Holly for a ride, so Rob and Holly agreed to meet at Sean's.

They went inside. "Nice house," Mads said. She'd been dying to see what Sean's house would look like, and it was fancier than she'd imagined. It looked as if it had been decorated professionally, walls painted mauve and lilac, a mix of modern, antique, and Asian pieces carefully placed throughout the airy rooms.

The girls saw seniors and juniors they recognized but didn't know well enough to talk to. Jane, the leggy blonde Sean had brought to the dance, held court in the dining room, sitting on top of the table with a drink in her hand. There seemed to be a lot of kids from other schools around. Sean had placed bowls of chips and salsa and M&Ms around the living room, and was serving screwdrivers along with the usual beer.

"I'm surprised Sean would bother to put food out," Lina said.

"Yeah," Holly agreed. "It seems kind of girly."

Mads shot them a dirty look. "Maybe he's just a good host. Anyway, I like his feminine side."

He emerged from the kitchen carrying a round of screwdrivers, two in each hand. He nodded at Mads as he distributed the drinks to Jane's friends.

"Hi, Sean," Mads said. She took the pose she'd been practicing all afternoon in the mirror, thrusting her right hip out and pouting.

"Hey, kid. Glad you could make it." He grinned at her. Wow. He was glad she could make it! Mads tried to think of something to say that would keep the conversation going. Something like, "Wouldn't miss it for the world." No, too stiff. "Thought I'd stop by on my way to the ten other parties I'm invited to." Hmm, not too believable. "I know my hair looks like I stuck my finger in a socket but it will be back to normal by Monday." No, probably not a good idea to draw attention to the hair.

Jane said, "Sean, can you get Tess a beer?" and he disappeared into the kitchen again. Too late. But Mads was sure she'd get another chance before the night was over.

"Let's go get a drink," Holly said, hoping to distract Mads from her early defeat.

"Good idea," Mads said. "Maybe Alex is in the kitchen."

Alex was in the kitchen, and so was most of the party. Holly spotted Rob by the fridge and waved. He pulled out four beers, one for each of them.

"Thanks," Holly said. She kissed him on the cheek.

"Thanks, Roberto," Mads said. She sashayed across the room to the kitchen table, where Alex sat with Mo and Jen.

"Hey, it's the kid!" Alex said. "Have a seat." He pushed his chair back so Mads could perch on his knee. She hesitated—sitting on his lap seemed so little-girlish, but on the other hand, it could be vampy. She decided it was vampy and sat down with her arm around his neck.

"Kid, you know Mo and Jen, don't you?" Alex asked.

"Hi. I'm Madison."

"How old are you, twelve?" Jen asked.

"Jen—" Mo nudged her.

"She's got to be at least in ninth grade, right kid?" Alex said. "I mean, you were at the winter dance and everything."

"I'm in tenth grade," Mads said.

"Wow, you're little," Jen said.

"Je-en," Mo said.

Mads was stung. Why was Jen picking on her? Maybe she liked Alex, too.

"Leave her alone, Jen," Alex said. "What are you drinking there? Beer? What's the matter, don't you like screwdrivers?"

Mads had never had a screwdriver before, though she had had vodka and cranberry juice, and it wasn't bad.

"Sure I like them," Mads said.

"Well, let's go get you one," Alex said. "I'm ready for another."

"Get me one, too," Jen said.

Alex didn't get one for Jen. He and Mads soon forgot all about Jen. He mixed up a couple of strong screwdrivers, heavy on the vodka, and led Mads out to the living room.

"Hey, how was that hamburger you had last week?" Mads asked.

"What?" Alex didn't know what she was talking about. Mads let it slide. The screwdriver was pretty good. It didn't taste much like vodka. Mads drank it down and

Alex got her another one. She felt a pleasant lightness at the top of her head. It made her feel goofy and brave. She wasn't intimidated by Alex or Jen or Jane or Sean or anyone. She could say whatever she wanted. And Alex seemed to think every word that came out of her mouth was just adorable.

"Do you think it's girly that Sean put out chips and snacks for us?" she asked Alex. They sat on the living room couch together, crammed between five other people, munching out. She reached into a bowl of chips and stuffed a few into her mouth.

"It's not girly," Alex said. "He's taking care of his peeps. 'Course, if he cut up carrot sticks and stuff, that would be girly." He chomped on another chip. "So tell me your life story, kid. I figure it's nice and short."

"You know, my name's not kid, it's Madison," Mads said.

"Yeah, I know, but I like calling you kid better. You don't mind, do you?"

She was actually starting to like it. "What should I call you? Baby? Al?"

"Whatever turns you on, kid."

"Listen, do you know Sean's middle name?"

"No," Alex said. "Why should I? Anyway, whatever it is, he doesn't like to tell."

"Huh. I wonder why?"

"It's probably embarrassing. Happens to the best of us. So, life story. You were born—"

"I was born in Berkeley, blah blah blah. Why don't you tell me yours?"

"Okay. I was born in SF, and I wish we'd never left. Don't you hate this crappy town?"

"I think it's pretty," Mads said. "But I love the city, too."

"Sure it's pretty, but it's so boring!" Alex said. "It has no edge."

"Well, you're a senior, right? So you won't be stuck here much longer. Where do you want to go to college?"

"NYU, if I get in. New York is where it's at."

"I've never been. My friend Holly has. She says SF is dorky compared to New York."

"She's right. SF is cool, but it's small-time."

"Hey, that sort of rhymes." Mads was a step or two behind in the conversation. "SF is dorky compared to New Yorky."

"*You're* dorky. Let me get you another one of those suckers. Oh wait, there's Sean." He held their plastic cups out to Sean, who was wading through the tangle of legs and scolding a girl for not using an ashtray. "Sean! Refills!" Alex ordered.

"Hey, man, I'm not a damn waiter," Sean said. He scowled at Alex. Mads took that opportunity to put Alex's hand on her thigh, to make Sean jealous. Sean didn't seem to notice. Opportunity lost. But somehow Mads didn't care that much. It seemed a lot more important to get ahold of another screwdriver and keep that fizzy feeling in her head.

Alex grinned at Mads, squeezed her thigh and shrugged. "Sheesh, what a grouch. I'll be right back."

Mads spotted Lina and Holly standing by the front door, talking to Rob. Rob was leaning close to Holly. They almost looked like boyfriend and girlfriend. *Go Boobmeister*, Mads thought. Looks like she'll be getting some action tonight. But what about Lina?

The front door opened and Jake walked in. Uh-oh— trouble? Good old Holly, she played it cool. She nodded at Jake and said hi, then turned back to Rob and kept talking. Jake actually orbited around the three of them for a few seconds, waiting for some kind of reaction. They ignored him. Finally Lina politely said something to him and pointed toward the kitchen. Mads thought she caught a stormy look cross Jake's face. What a jerk. He treats Holly like dirt and expects her to come back for more?

Ah, here was Alex, back with four cups. "Sean's running out of vodka, so I got us each two drinks," he said.

"Smart," Mads thought she said, but it came out sounding like "Schmart." She giggled.

● ● ●

When Walker arrived, Lina was relieved in spite of herself. Rob and Holly were being nice, including her in their conversation and everything, but it was obvious they were really into each other and she found their coded love talk boring. None of her other friends were at the party, except for Mads, and she was busy giggling and drinking herself silly with Alex.

Lina started to get that feeling again, like she was floating above the room, watching everyone else have a good time but not participating herself. In a weird way, the party was more interesting from a distance. As if, floating invisibly over their heads, she could see the truth behind all the banality and bull everybody was spouting. She pretended she was seeing the party through Dan's eyes, dispassionately, analytically, like an adult. People were beginning to get drunk, and they weren't making a whole lot of sense.

Lina followed Walker to the kitchen for a fresh bottle of beer. "I didn't know you were going to be here," he said. "I would have asked you to come but I figured you were busy."

Lina was flattered that he thought she had such a full social life, and decided to let him keep thinking it. "Oh, you know. Mads and Holly wanted to come. . . ."

Walker clinked the neck of his beer bottle against hers in a toast. "So what's new on the scene? I checked your

187

blog today. Beats 'Nuclear Autumn' by a mile. What does old Danny boy think of it? It's an IHD project, right?"

Danny boy? "He likes it so far."

"I was reading an old issue of the *Seer* from last fall, and I saw a picture of you on the JV hockey team. You guys were pretty good this year, seven and three. Bet you make Varsity next fall."

"Thanks." Walker started talking about last week's girls' basketball game, but Lina couldn't stop thinking about Dan, about his house, her poem with his scratched-out handwriting on it, and the secret they shared. She wished she could tell Walker about it, even though she knew that was stupid. Walker would probably be shocked. It gave Lina an oddly warm, good feeling to know that she had a shocking secret and no one suspected it. She could freak Walker out if she wanted to. She had the power. She simply chose not to use it. It was too much for a mere boy like Walker to handle.

"Hey. Didn't think I'd see *you* here."

Lina turned around. A girl was speaking to her. She looked very familiar, but it took Lina a second to place her. "Ramona?"

"What, you don't recognize me? You've only known me for five years."

Lina had never expected to see Ramona at Sean's, and even more amazing, Ramona had come to the party without her usual goth drag. Her raven-black hair was pulled back in a ponytail, and she wasn't wearing much makeup, maybe some lip gloss. Instead of her usual long black dress she wore jeans and a t-shirt.

"What are you doing here?" Lina asked.

"I live next door. I saw Sean was having a party so I figured I'd crash it. You?"

"Sean invited Mads," Lina said. She paused. Walker said, "I'll see you later, Lina," and walked away.

"I hope I didn't scare away your boyfriend," Ramona said.

"He's not my boyfriend," Lina said. "And anyway, you look a little less scary than usual, no offense."

"I think I look scarier than usual," Ramona said. "But do you know how long it takes to put on all that makeup? Sometimes I just don't have the energy. And without the makeup, the clothes look all wrong."

"So why do you do it?" Lina asked.

"It's cool," Ramona said. "And it looks beautiful. At least I think so."

Lina just nodded. *To each her own.*

"So, who do you know here?" Ramona asked after a brief, uncomfortable silence.

"Nobody," Lina said. "Just Walker and Holly and Mads. And Rob, I guess."

"That's not nobody."

"Who do you know?"

"Just Sean. And you. But Sean doesn't really pay attention to me. My mom knows his mom, but I don't think he knows my name."

"I get the feeling he's bad with names," Lina said.

They stood in silence for a few more minutes, the party clattering around them. Ramona lit a cigarette. Lina sighed. Holly was busy with Rob, and Mads was busy with Alex, and Walker had gone off somewhere, and there she was with Ramona. It was weird, but she almost felt grateful to Ramona. She was someone to talk to besides Walker. Or not talk to, as it turned out.

"Long as I'm here, I might as well have a beer," Ramona said. She opened the fridge and grabbed a can. "Want to go out on the porch and watch the stoners make fools of themselves?"

"Okay."

Mads rested her head on the back of the couch and stared at a plaster design on the living room ceiling. It blurred, then came back into focus. Wow. She was actually in Sean's house! It really hit her now. Sean's very own house! Where he grew up and did whatever private things he did. Mads was dying to see the upstairs. What did Sean's room look like? Did he have posters? What color was his toothbrush?

"Hey, kid, you haven't finished your last drink yet,"

Alex said, staring into her plastic cup.

Mads lifted her head. Across the room, Sean fiddled with the stereo. He turned around and surveyed the party, his eyes resting on Mads for a split second. She waved to him. "Great party!" she yelled, but the music was loud and he couldn't hear her.

"What?" he shouted.

Jane suddenly appeared and bumped her hip against his. He grabbed her and kissed her. They danced a little together. Sean never looked back at Mads to find out what she'd yelled to him. Probably just as well. It was lame anyway.

"Let's go upstairs," Mads said, getting woozily to her feet. "Come on. I want to see the upstairs." She'd show Sean.

"Sure thing, kiddo," Alex said. Kiddo. He thought he was so smooth. Mads liked him. But he was no Sean.

Did I just say that out loud? Mads wondered. A glance at Alex's tranquil, stoned face told her no, thank god.

Alex followed her up the stairs. "Which one is Sean's room?" she asked.

"Down there." Alex pointed down the hall. "But I don't think Sean wants us to go in there."

"I just want to see what it looks like." Mads opened the door and peeked in. It wasn't at all like she'd pictured it. There was a modern steel-framed bed with a woolly beige cover, a big red-and-blue Persian rug, and a spare black desk. On the wall hung a framed poster of a Kandinsky painting. Not very boyish. The only sign that Sean lived there was a bookcase filled with schoolbooks, sports trophies, and a few framed photos. Huh.

"It looks like his mom decorated it for him," Mads said.

"She did. She's pretty uptight about house stuff. But he's more of a neat freak than you'd expect, too."

"Interesting," Mads said. She stopped in the hall bathroom. "Gotta pee," she told Alex.

"I'll wait for you," Alex said.

Mads closed the door, peed, then checked out the medicine cabinet. Sean used a brown, wooden, natural-bristle toothbrush. She never would have guessed. And he shaved with an electric razor. And he used acne cream! Prescription acne cream! Mads read the label. "Sean Herman Benedetto." His middle name was Herman? Somehow it didn't quite fit. Mads shrugged. She knew that once she got used to it, Herman would become her second-favorite boys' name, after Sean.

Alex knocked on the door. "Kid? Are you okay?"

She opened the door. "Fine. What's next?" She wandered down the hall to the biggest room, a beautiful master bedroom with a sitting area and a fireplace. Must be his parents' room.

"Wow. This is fancy," Mads said. She sat on the bed. Sean's mother's bed. The cover was blue silk. Beneath her feet was a white rug with a black swirl pattern on it. Swirl, swirl, swirl . . .

Alex sat beside her. He kissed her forehead, then her cheek, then her mouth. "Hey, kid—"

Mads leaned back until she was lying on the bed. She had to. She felt so dizzy . . .

"All right," Alex murmured, kissing her. She turned her face away. No! She needed air! He definitely should not block her access to air.

"What's wrong?" Alex asked.

"I feel dizzy," Mads said.

"Uh-oh." Alex stood up. "You know, you look a little pale. Here, sit up."

He helped Mads sit up, but that didn't help. Alex had a bad feeling about this. He could see where this was headed. And he didn't want to be around when Sean freaked out.

"Hey, kid, you'll be okay," Alex said. "I'll go get you some Coke to settle your stomach. Be right back." He hurried downstairs.

Mads stared at the swirling rug pattern. Her stomach churned. How many vodkas did she have? Why did she have to drink so many? Why didn't she finish her stir-fry at dinner like M.C. told her to? Ugh, she felt so sick. . . .

"Hey, what are you doing in here?" Sean stood in the doorway. "This is my mom's room. Nobody's supposed to be in here. Come on, kid, let's go."

Mads leaned forward. She meant to stand up. She meant to walk out of there, just like he wanted her to. But she never got that far. She crouched down and puked all over the carpet.

"Great. This is just great," Sean muttered. Mads lay crumpled on the rug, vomit in her hair, moaning. Sean helped her up. "This is why I don't like kids coming to my parties." He led Mads to the bathroom. "If you're going to hurl, do it in there. In the toilet. Not all over my mom's rug."

He closed the door. Mads crawled into the bathtub. She was still dizzy. Her head throbbed and her stomach churned. She was afraid she might puke again.

She'd wanted Sean to notice her. Well, he noticed her all right. Now if she could just find a way to make him forget it.

20 Ouch, That's Gotta Hurt

I need to get something from the car," Rob said. He and Holly were sitting on the front steps leading up to Sean's house, sipping beer and stealing kisses between sips. "Want to come with me?"

"Sure." Holly rose to her feet. Was this it? Going out to the car—and then what? "What do you have to get?"

"I left a joint in the glove compartment," Rob confided. "Maybe we can take a hit before we bring it back to share with the teeming masses."

She followed him out to a big black Suburban. "Mom's SUV," he explained a little sheepishly. Well, it was sure big enough for whatever anyone might want to do. Rob opened the door for her, and she climbed inside. Then he got into the driver's seat, reached across her to the glove compartment and got the joint. He lit it with the car's lighter. "Want a hit?"

"No, thanks." Holly had smoked pot before, but she didn't like the woozy way it made her feel. Whatever was going to happen next, she didn't want to feel woozy. She wanted to feel good, and to remember it.

He took a hit, leaned back, and exhaled. Holly watched the smoke cloud the car and breathed in. Maybe a little bit of second-hand smoke wouldn't hurt.

Rob put out the joint and stuffed it in a matchbox. Then he stroked Holly's hair. "You've got great hair," he drawled, a little stoned now. "Really great hair."

"Thanks." That seemed to be a popular line with the boys. She waited to see what would happen next. He closed his eyes and moved his face toward hers. His lips missed hers by a half an inch, bumping the bottom of her nose. They laughed, and he opened his eyes.

"Let's try that again." He managed to find her lips. He was a surprisingly stiff kisser this time. But maybe it was the weed. Did pot make you a clumsy kisser? Might be something to look into on the Web site.

Maybe it was up to her to do something. She remembered the *Cosmo* article. What had they suggested? Something about chocolate or whipped cream—not very practical at the moment. What else? Nibble his lips to drive a guy wild. So she started to kiss him more passionately, and he relaxed a little. Then she carefully nipped at his bottom lip. He giggled as if he'd been tickled.

"That's great," he murmured. It was working! She nibbled some more. "Mmmm," he said. "Nick was right."

What? Nick? Was right about what? She started, mid-nibble, and bit down a little too hard.

"Ow!" Rob yelped. His hand flew to his lip. It was bleeding. "What was that for?"

"What are you talking about?" Holly demanded. "What did Nick say?"

"Nothing! He just said you were really hot, that's all."

"Hot how?"

Rob stared at her, a little afraid. "Have you lost it? You nearly bit my lip off!"

"Hot how?"

"You know, when you're fooling around and stuff."

"How would Nick know what I'm like when I'm fooling around?" Holly demanded.

"Well, didn't you—I mean, he told me—"

"*He* told you!" Holly couldn't believe it. Nick was the

one who spread the rumors about the two of them at the Christmas party? Those rumors that were one hundred percent lies? And Rob believed them?

And what about Jake? Did Rob believe him, too?

Was that why Rob wanted to be with her? Because of her rep? Because Nick said she'd put out—and everybody else said so, too?

"Do you guys talk about me a lot?" Holly asked. "What else did he tell you?"

Rob looked nervous. "Well, uh, nothing—"

He clammed up because he was scared. And he had good reason to be. Holly was furious.

"You know what? You shouldn't listen to your friend Nick. He's a liar. And so is Jake. Maybe you're all liars!"

She jumped out of the car and ran back to the party. She stopped outside the front door of the house and took a deep breath. No crying. Not at the party. Not until she was safely in her car.

She'd thought he liked her for real. But now she had to wonder.

He'd never seemed to notice her before Mariska's party—when Jake was saying she'd put out for *him*, too.

Maybe that was all he wanted. Maybe he was using her! What if she had fooled around with him just now in the car? Would she have ever heard from him again?

# 21 A Night to Forget

To:	linaonme
From:	Your daily horoscope

HERE IS TODAY'S HOROSCOPE: CANCER: You're a very sensitive person. It will come in handy later, when you're talking about this day in group therapy.

Dude, that was so funny," Mo said to Barton. Lina and Ramona were sitting on the porch, watching the stoners. "I thought I lost my keys and they—heh heh—were in my pocket the whole time!"

Mo and Barton cracked up. "No way!" Barton said. "They were in your pocket?" He could hardly speak, he was laughing so hard.

"What was I thinking? Stoners must be the most boring people on the planet," Ramona said. She set down her empty beer bottle. "I've had enough. Guess I'll go home."

To her surprise, Lina didn't want Ramona to go home. Not just yet. If Ramona left, what would Lina do?

"You want to come with me?" Ramona asked. "It's just next door. I could show you the Museum."

Oh. The Museum of Dan. Lina cringed. "No, that's okay," she said. "Maybe some other time." It was one thing to hang around with Ramona at a party where she hardly knew anybody. It was another thing to look at Ramona's collection of stuff Dan threw out. That was where she drew the line.

"Suit yourself," Ramona said. "Have fun with the Normals." She smirked, walked down the steps, and disappeared in the dark. Lina saw her shadow cross the lighted porch next door. So, Ramona had a house. And parents. And a face under all that makeup. Lina still didn't want to be friends with her. But somehow, in spite of herself, she thought it might be happening.

"There you are." Lina found Mads in an upstairs bathroom, lying in the tub. "I've been looking all over for you. What happened?"

Mads pressed her cheek against the cool white ceramic, slowly coming to her senses. "Lina," she sobbed. "I'm so embarrassed."

"Oh, no," Lina said. "Was that your puke Sean was cleaning up?"

"Uh-huh. I feel awful." She reached one arm out to Lina. "Help me sit up."

Sean peeked into the bathroom. "Hey, kid. Are you okay?" He nodded at Lina. "Everything under control here?"

"I think so," Lina said.

Sean tossed Mads a large white towel. "Here. In case you want to wash up or something." He disappeared, leaving Lina and Mads alone.

Lina grabbed Mads' hands and helped her out of the tub. "God, why did Sean have to see me this way?" Mads moaned. Her clothes were rumpled, her hair sticky and stinking of vodka and puke. "I wanted him to notice me, but not like this. Obviously."

"It's okay," Lina said. "Come on, you'll feel better after you've washed up a little."

Lina helped Mads wash her face and rinse out her mouth and the sticky strands of her hair. Mads draped a limp arm over Lina's back and let her head fall on her shoulder, heavy as a rock.

"Where's Holly?" Mads asked. "I want to go home."

"She disappeared with Rob a little while ago," Lina said. "Let's go find her."

Downstairs, Holly darted from room to room, searching for her friends. She didn't want to abandon them, but she couldn't stand to stay at the party another minute. They found her sitting on the stairs.

"I think we'd better go home, Holly," Lina said. "Mads isn't feeling well."

Holly got to her feet and helped Lina support Mads. "Mads, what's wrong?"

"Too many screwdrivers," Lina said. "Let's go."

They left the house and started down the steps to the street. Rob burst through the front door and called out, "Holly! Wait!"

Holly started to run down the stone steps. Lina and Mads kept up the best they could.

"Holly, Rob's calling you," Lina said.

"I know," Holly said. She didn't look back. She knew his lip must be swollen. People would ask him about it— or draw their own conclusions. She wanted to get out of there before more rumors started buzzing.

She found the VW and started it before Mads and Lina had a chance to get in. Mads collapsed onto the back seat, and Lina sat in the front. "What's wrong, Holly?"

"Nothing. Just total disaster." She pulled away and they drove in silence down the street. Lina could tell Holly was very upset, and she was afraid to push too hard for information. But Holly started talking again after a block or two. She told Lina what had happened in Rob's car. Mads sat slumped in the back, eyes closed, listening.

"I was really starting to like him," Holly said. "He seemed so nice! But he's just as bad as Jake or any other guy. He thinks I'm a slut! That's why he wanted to go out with me. Nick told him I'd do whatever! And what really kills me is that's all made up."

"I don't get it," Mads said. "Everybody thinks you're sexy. You *are* sexy. What's the big deal?"

"Mads, you're the one who's always talking about trying to seem older and how cool it is to be sexy," Holly said. "You and your stupid tips. I was trying to nibble Rob's lips when I got so upset I ended up biting him! God, I can't believe I did that."

"It's not my fault you bit him too hard," Mads said.

"This whole thing is your fault!" Holly cried. "You're the one who wrote 'Boobmeister Holly' on that quiz in the first place. That's what started it all." Her knuckles went white on the steering wheel. She couldn't stand feeling so out of control.

Mads started crying. She'd never seen Holly this angry before. Lina sat quietly, trying to piece it all together. Holly always seemed so strong, as if nothing ever got to her. But now it was pretty clear that all the teasing and the talk really hurt her.

"Mads didn't mean to start rumors about you," Lina said. "She didn't know Autumn would post the quiz on her blog, and the whole thing would blow up in our faces. Mads was just goofing around and you know it."

Holly felt bad. She knew it wasn't Mads' fault, but

sometimes Mads did such stupid things . . . "I know. I'm sorry, Mads. I'm just so . . . I can't stand it! I hate the way people talk about me, the way they look at me. I can't stand that I have no control over how people think of me, no matter what I do, all they ever see is my tits! You should be glad you're such a little pipsqueak, Mads. It's better than being treated like a blow-up sex doll."

"Can I have some Kleenex?" Mads reached over the front seat, hand out. Lina stuck a wad of tissues in it. "Thanks." Mads blew her nose.

"I didn't want to hurt you, Holly. I thought you kind of liked it when I teased you."

"I know. I do. Sort of."

"From now on I'll only talk to you or about you as if you are some kind of very serious nuclear physicist."

"That's okay, Mads. You can tease me. But you know, this whole experience thing is such a scam. Nobody at school is as experienced as they say they are. They're all full of it. Like Jake. And you should have seen Rob tonight. Mr. Cool. Your dog Boris kisses better than he does."

"But what about Sean?" Mads said. "He said I wasn't experienced enough! I still think that's why he won't go out with me."

"Well, now he's got an even better reason," Lina said.

Mads leaned back against the seat, still a little drunk.

Holly was right. Mads could finally see it now. Everybody pretended to know what they were doing. But nobody knew anything. Half the answers to the Dating Game questionnaires were made up. Even Alex . . . maybe the reason he couldn't wait to run off and get a hamburger was because he wasn't sure of himself with her. With *her*! And what about Sean? How experienced was he?

Sean. God, why did she have to get sick at his house of all places?

"You know, he came into the bathroom and asked if I was okay," she said. In her memory that moment became something intimate between them, even though Lina was there. "He gave me a towel and said, 'Are you okay?' I think that shows he cares about me! He could have just left me there."

Holly knocked her forehead on the top of the steering wheel. This was too pathetic.

"Mads, you are so deluded," Holly said. "Just because he didn't want you to mess up his mom's bedroom—" She gave up, knowing it was hopeless. Mads clung to the dream of Sean the way some people played the lottery. It was a long shot, but she couldn't let go as long as the chance was there.

"At least he'll really remember me now," Mads said.

"Yeah, every time he sees the stain on his mother's rug," Holly said.

"Maybe you should keep your distance from him for a little while," Lina suggested. "You know, so he won't associate you with being sick. Let the memory fade a little."

"If it ever will," Holly said. "It's really hard to get the vomit smell out of a rug."

Mads clutched her head in her hands. "You guys! You're not helping!"

"All right, Mads," Holly said. "One day, when you and Sean are married and looking back at your wacky teen years, you'll laugh about this."

"Ah." Mads closed her eyes and let the image sink in. It was their fiftieth wedding anniversary and their mansion was filled with visiting grandchildren. Sean was telling them all the funny story about how Grandma ruined Great-Grandma's swirly white rug. "That's much better."

"Lina, what did you do while Mads and I battled it out for the title of Drama Queen?" Holly asked.

"I saw Ramona without her makeup," Lina said.

"She was there?" Mads said. "How did she get invited?"

"She lives next door."

"How did she look without all that gunk?" Holly asked.

"Normal," Lina said.

22 So Long, Boobmeister

HERE IS TODAY'S HOROSCOPE: CAPRICORN: Sure, you're bombarded with junk, but you've got to learn to sift through it carefully so you don't miss the gold. Someone is trying to get through to you, but you keep mistaking his e-mails for spam.

To: hollygolitely
From: flappie
Re: please don't delete me!
Holly—I'm really sorry I upset you. I didn't mean to, I swear! I
    want to see you again. I know Nick's a big liar and I
    don't care what anybody says about you—I think you
    are so cool. I told everybody at the party that you
    punched me in the lip when I tried to kiss you. They

were all saying what a big prude you are. Pretty fickle
crowd. My lip's already healing and anyway I don't care
about that. I just want to see you again. Please? Can we
meet for coffee after school on Friday and talk? Maybe
dinner or a movie after that, if you feel like it? Say yes!
—Rob

"I scanned it for sarcasm and insincerity," Holly said.
She was sitting with Lina and Mads at Vineland after
school on Wednesday, dissecting Rob's e-mail for the
tenth time that week. "I think it was clean."

"So what are you going to do?" Mads asked.

"I don't know. It's hard for me to trust him after Jake."

"Holly, do you like him?" Lina asked.

Holly looked as if she'd been stuck with a needle. "I
think so. Which sucks."

"No, it's a good thing," Lina reminded her. "Try to
keep that in mind."

"The question is, does he really like me?"

Lina grinned at Mads and gave Holly a piece of
paper. "You walked right into our little scheme," she said.

"What's this?"

"It's a quiz," Mads said. "Lina and I wrote it just for you."

<u>Does He Really Like You?</u>
for Holly by Lina and Mads

1. Someone is spreading nasty rumors about you at a party.
   You leave the room. Your special guy:

   a ▶ Doesn't move

   b ▶ Adds to the rumors

   c ▶ Follows you out of the room to see if you're okay

2. You spot him sitting with friends in the school library. He:

   a ▶ Ignores you

   b ▶ Gives you a half-hearted nod

   c ▶ Smiles at you and waves

3. A school dance is coming up. He:

   a ▶ Asks another girl to be his date

   b ▶ Doesn't ask you but figures he'll see you there

   c ▶ Asks you to go with him

4. At the dance, a jerk tries to embarrass you. Your date:

   a ▶ Leaves you in disgrace

   b ▶ Pretends it never happened

   c ▶ Stands by you and takes you out for milkshakes later

5. While making out in his car, you accidentally bite his lip. He:

   a ▶ Never wants to talk to you again

   b ▶ Tells everyone at the party what a crazy bitch you are

   c ▶ Runs after you, tries to stop you from leaving, and

▶ **immediately e-mails you, begging to see you again**

Answer Key: If you answered c to these questions (and you better have!), the situation is clear: <u>Rob really likes you!</u>

Holly laughed. "Thanks, you guys. It's weird to see your life in quiz form. But very revealing."

"We just think you shouldn't be afraid," Mads said.

"All right," Holly said. "I will take a chance on Rob. That's settled. Anything else up for discussion?"

"I got something in the mail from Sean!" Mads waved another piece of paper in front of them. Lina snatched it.

"This is a bill from a carpet-cleaning service," she said. "Seventy-five dollars."

"I know." Mads took it back and carefully replaced it in its envelope. "I'll treasure it forever."

"Are you going to pay it?" Holly asked.

"No," Mads said. "If I paid it, I'd have to send it back to the carpet cleaners. And I want to keep it."

"Sean will really appreciate that," Holly said. "Before I forget, can you both come over to my house to work on our IHD paper tomorrow?" Their final report was due on Friday. Mads was in charge of gathering all the data, Holly was going to analyze it, and Lina's job was to write it up.

"Sounds good," Lina said.

"I've already charted most of the info," Mads said. "I

hope Dan's ready for good look at the sordid underbelly of RSAGE."

"I'll kind of miss reading those questionnaires, even if they were a pack of lies," Holly said. "I think we should keep the blog going. It doesn't matter if the project is finished. We can still make matches."

"And we can still make up quizzes to find out the deep dark secrets of our classmates," Mads said. "That's my favorite part."

"Let's definitely keep it," Lina said.

"Good," Holly said. "In other news?"

"The latest issue of *Inchworm* just came out." Lina tossed a thin booklet on the table. It was printed on shiny paper, the cover illustrated with a worm crawling across a bloody ruler which, Lina concluded, was also a razor blade. "See page thirteen."

Holly turned to page thirteen and read aloud. 'Lost Cause' by Ramona Fernandez:

In love, I suffered alone
Or so I thought
Then I found you
Fellow-sufferer and
Friend.
We each tilt at our own windmill, alone,
But knowing you're out there, tilting too,
Gives me strength.

"I don't get it," Holly finished.

"It's about me," Lina said. "She likes Dan. I like Dan. I guess knowing I like him too spurs her on. Or something."

"Is that a good thing?" Mads asked. "I mean, only one of you can have him, right? One at most. If you're lucky."

"I don't know," Lina said, and she was genuinely confused by the poem. It seemed to be a challenge and a gesture of friendship simultaneously.

"Ramona's weird," Holly said. "Luckily nobody reads *Inchworm*. So we don't have to worry about what it means."

"That's what I figure," Lina said.

"Lina, why don't you forget about Dan?" Mads said. "Walker really likes you, and he's a fox."

"You could give him a chance," Holly said. "I mean, what's the point in pining over Dan like this? It's okay to have a crush and everything, but you've got to be realistic."

"I know," Lina said. "You guys are right. It's unrealistic and a waste of time."

And part of Lina knew that was true. But she didn't care. She loved Dan more and more every day. She thought about him constantly. She thought about the secret between them. She'd keep the secret, even from her best friends.

But she couldn't live on the secret alone. She had to see him, had to kiss him, had to have a minute alone with him, had to hear him tell her how he really felt.

And her chance was coming. Because Dan had a

secret, too—and Lina knew what it was.

She'd found it just last night. Scanning Web sites for ideas for the Dating Game, she came across a personal ad. A twenty-four-year-old man named *beauregard*, a high-school teacher, looking for love. And right at the top, Dan's picture.

"You guys are right," she said again. "I should forget about him. I will."

But she couldn't. And she knew she wouldn't.

"So, how does it look?" Rob asked. He stuck out his lower lip. "All healed?"

It was late Friday afternoon, and he and Holly were sitting on a bench by the waterfront. Holly studied his lip. No sign of a scar. It was a cute, plump little lip. "Looks fine to me. Good enough to eat." She gnashed her teeth.

He pulled away in mock horror. "Don't worry," she said. "I'm on a lip-free diet."

"Good. Because my poor lip has been recuperating, and it needs some exercise to get back up to full strength."

Holly leaned close to him. "Let's test it out."

They kissed. Why did Holly ever say that Mads' dog Boris kissed better? It wasn't true. Not even close.

They broke apart. Holly rested her head on Rob's shoulder. She felt warm and happy. She had a sudden urge to run her fingers through his thick, choppy brown hair. Her new boyfriend's beautiful hair. She understood now why boys were always telling girls they have nice hair. When you liked someone, you wanted to touch his hair. Or maybe boys just couldn't think of anything better to say. Yes, that was more likely.

"You busy this weekend?" he asked.

"No," Holly said.

"You are now."

Class: Interpersonal Human Development:
The Dating Game: Who's More Sex-Crazed, Boys or Girls?
Final Report
by Holly Anderson, Madison Markowitz, Lina Ozu

After administering several tests, quizzes, and polls to the students of RSAGE, we must reluctantly come to the conclusion that our original hypothesis was wrong. We assumed that boys were more focused on sex than girls. Our test results indicate that at the very least, girls are just as interested in sex as boys. In every poll and every quiz, the results were close to 50/50.

It is our field work that forces us to conclude that, in fact, girls care about sex more than boys. They talk about it more. They read about it more. They think about it more. Yes, this is anecdotal evidence. We are girls; we don't get to hear what boys talk about when they are alone together. Our scientific technique is not exactly airtight here. All we can say is, we know what we know.

If you insist, we could write up a report on the tests we conducted in the field. It is highly recommended, however, for the sake of your own sanity, that you do not insist. Just take our word for it. We wouldn't lie.

Conclusion: Girls are more obsessed with sex than boys.

"Excellent job, girls," Dan said after Lina had read their report to the class. Mads and Holly gathered up the charts and graphs they had made and returned to their seats.

"I think we aced it," Holly whispered.

"Me, too," Lina said.

"Does anyone have any questions or comments about this project?" Dan asked the class.

Karl Levine raised his hand. "Yeah, I do. If girls are so obsessed with sex, how come I can't get one to put out for me?"

The class laughed. Mads rolled her eyes. Stupid Karl. She turned to a blank page in her notebook and started doodling.

"Your listening comprehension needs work, Karl," Dan said. "Since you raised your hand, are you ready to read us your final paper?"

Karl went to the front of the room and started reading from his magnum opus, "Lara Croft versus Xena— Which One's Hotter?" Mads tuned out and started scribbling.

Holly Driscoll Anderson and Robert ? Safran

A lot of things had changed since the beginning of the semester. Holly had a new boyfriend. And the only person who still called her the Boobmeister was Mads. And Holly didn't really mind that. Spring was coming, and it was looking good.

Lina Alice Ozu and Walker ? Moore

Maybe Lina didn't like him that much yet but he sure liked her. Mads kind of hoped Lina would come around. And she refused to write Lina's name next to Daniel Dorkhead Shulman's.

Madison Emily Markowitz and Sean Herman Benedetto

Only a few weeks earlier, Sean didn't know she existed. Now she knew his middle name! Okay, so nothing big had happened between them yet—but Mads was getting closer. She could feel it.

I, Madison Emily Markowitz, do solemnly vow that by the end of the school year, Sean Herman Benedetto will be mine.

Is that really Rebecca?" Holly said. "I don't think I've ever seen her eat carbs before."

Holly, Mads and Lina sat in the lunchroom that afternoon, watching Rebecca Hulse and David Kim feed each other spaghetti. Rebecca, a skinny blond alpha girl, was normally a bit of an ice princess, but hunky David seemed to have melted her. She cooed and slurped up a forkful of pasta, tomato sauce splattering her chin.

"I'm not sure spaghetti is the best choice for love feeding," Lina said. "Wouldn't strawberries work better?"

"He's turned her to mush," Holly said. "I didn't think that was possible."

"For a split second I thought she wasn't cool anymore," Mads said. "But then I realized—all she did was change the definition of cool. I'm suddenly desperate to grab a boy and start slapping spaghetti all over him."

Rebecca and David nibbled a long strand of pasta, each starting at one end until their lips met in the middle.

"I matched them myself," Holly said. The Dating Game blog had a matchmaking section, and Rebecca had submitted an application. When Holly chose David for her, she was afraid Rebecca would reject him. "Now they're like Lady and the Tramp. The question is, which is which?" Holly paused to bite into her sandwich, but her eyes traveled back up to David. "He's cute," she said. "Why didn't I ever notice it before?"

"Because you have Rob," Mads said. "Rob's cute, too. He blocked you from noticing other guys."

"Well, it's not working anymore," Holly said.

"What do you mean it's not working anymore? Rob is the greatest boyfriend!" Lina said. "I thought you really liked him."

"I do like him," Holly said. "But something's not right. . . ."

"Hmmm . . . I see trouble clouding those baby blues." Sebastiano Altman-Peck stared into Holly's eyes late Monday afternoon. Holly's locker was next to his, so she saw him at least twice a day. He was part of her routine, like brushing her teeth.

"The Great Sebastiano sees all. The patient is experiencing acute symptoms of severe Sebastiano-withdrawal."

"Excuse me, Great Sebastiano, while I turn away from your penetrating gaze." Holly dialed the combination on her lock. "I want to get my books and get out of here. What's Sebastiano-withdrawal, anyway?"

"You haven't seen me for two whole days. It makes you cranky. Don't worry, it's perfectly normal." Sebastiano rummaged through his locker until he found a long red scarf. "There you are," he said to the scarf as he wrapped it around his neck. He slammed his locker shut and leaned against it. "Now. I sense you have love trouble. I want the dirt."

"There's no dirt," Holly said.

Sebastiano closed his eyes and rubbed his temples like a mind-reader. "The Great Sebastiano sees a hunky brown-haired boy . . . a red baseball cap . . . a pair of plastic swim goggles . . . Could it be—? Yes, it's star swimmer and Holly-adorer Rob Safran." He opened his eyes to confront Holly. "You might as well confess. I'll get it out of you sooner or later."

"Okay," Holly said. "Something is bothering me just a microbit. One teeny, tiny little thing that's not the least bit important at all."

"Ah-ha," Sebastiano said. "The Great Sebastiano is always right. And that tiny little thing would be—? It's the red baseball cap, isn't it? It makes your boyfriend look like Ronald McDonald. Which is too bad, because he's a hottie when his hair isn't flattened into a heinous fringe around his head."

"He promised to give up the cap," Holly said. "But

there's something else. Before he kisses me he says, `Do you mind if I kiss you?' Every single time."

"Really? That's uptight of him. Have you tried ordering him to stop? Or are *you* too uptight?"

"I am not!" Holly said.

"You're just chicken," Sebastiano said. "Hmmm . . . Here's my diagnosis. What you've got here is a Boy Who Likes You Too Much. He likes you so much he's afraid he'll do something wrong. His love for you has turned him into a wimp."

"Is there a cure?" Holly said. "I *really* like him. And he's only being nice."

"Right. Nice. Nothing sexier than nice." Sebastiano watched all the kids streaming out of the school's main door. "What about Mo Basri?" he said, mentioning a friend of Sean's. "I saw him checking you out the other day. Don't underestimate your appeal, Holly. You're smart, you're sweet, but you have a dab of eau-de-bad-girl behind your ear, if you know what I mean."

Holly paused. "Mo Basri was really checking me out?"

"Watched you walk from here to the gym for three straight minutes without taking his eyes off you," Sebastiano said.

Holly let this sink in. After a long winter, spring was here. Rebirth. New possibilities. Love in the air and all that. Maybe it was time for a change . . . in boyfriends.